How Hackleburg Became a Thirteen-Pie Church

How Hackleburg Became a Thirteen-Pie Church

BY RILEY B. CASE

Where joy finds a voice
1.888.273.4JOY
http://www.ajoyin.com

How Hackleburg Became a Thirteen-Pie Church
by Riley Case
Copyright © October 2004 by Riley B. Case
Reprinted 2016
Ajoyin Publishing

ISBN: 978-1-60920-112-8

Ajoyin Publishing
P.O. Box 342
Three Rivers, MI 49093
269-273-3600
www.ajoyin.com

To

*The people of Union Chapel, Springhill,
New Corydon, Claypool, Mount Pleasant,
Pleasant Grove, Ashley, Hudson, Elkhart Calvary,
Union City Wesley, the Marion District,
and St. Luke's Kokomo*

Table of Contents

Preface:
The History of the History of the Hackleburg Church

T here is, somewhere in the archives of Indiana Methodism at DePauw University, a folder marked "Hackleburg." It is reported—though no one has checked recently to know if this is really so—that the folder contains an official history of the church, whatever revision that might be, as well as several programs of Homecoming Sundays (none dated later than 1943) and minutes of the Ladies' Aid Society from 1931–1935.

There is not too much to learn about the Hackleburg church from that folder, or for that matter, from any number of written histories that show up from time to time around the church. There is a copy of a history in the right-hand drawer of the Sunday school secretary's desk, where it is usually noticed when someone is looking for an eraser or trying to find the attendance book for the FaHoCha

(Faith-Hope-Charity) Sunday school class. A copy lies gathering dust in a box marked "church history" in Annabelle Martin's closet. Annabelle is listed every year in the church directory as head of the history committee, a committee that has not met now—so far as anybody knows—since Pastor Jacobs was at the church in the 1980s.

Pastor Jacobs wanted the committee to get together and so they did. It was a cold day in March, and Annabelle served the most delicious ginger muffins to Pastor Jacobs, Mary Hooley and Margaret Strawser. They had a delightful two hours commenting on former church members and whatever happened to them, and on present church members and how the grandchildren were doing. At the end of the two hours, they agreed that they had nothing more to add to the official history of the church at that time.

The best that anyone can figure, the first history was written in 1924 when Marybelle Hasselbaum felt the story needed to be told about how her father, Harley Littlejohn, was converted in a great revival and started the church back in 1876; and how her mother, Bertha Winteregg Littlejohn, led the cause of Temperance and Morality and Decency in the community and started Hackleburg's first Women's Foreign Missionary Society; and how she, Marybelle Hasselbaum, took up the cause when her mother finally passed to be with Jesus.

A year or so later an addendum to that history was written when Wilbur Littlejohn, Bertha's first cousin (double-first cousin, actually), wrote some corrections or additions to the history, pointing out that his father Hank Littlejohn was also converted in the great revival in 1876 and had been responsible for construction of the first church building in 1882, and his mother, Gertie Winteregg Littlejohn, babysat with a number of preachers' kids through the years.

Wilbur also added the account of the wonderful new church building that had been built in 1916 and how the indoor toilets were added in 1926, during which time he was a trustee. An official ("official" meaning it was authorized by the Official Board and recorded in the church minutes) History Committee functioned sometime during the 1940s. At that time Homecoming programs were gathered, a number of old photos (an amazing number of which featured Marybelle Hasselbaum) were contributed and placed in a history box, and there was comment about how everyone enjoyed the chicken-and-noodle dinners. The chicken and noodle dinners were mentioned several other times in the history and seem to be what the church was mostly noted for for a number of years. There was also mention of Lush Larkin, generous patron, who bequeathed the church and the town land for the park; Susanna, faithful Methodist dog; and the names of the officers down through the years of the Woman's Society.

Sometime in the 1950s Rev. Jonathan Bell, in reading this history, realized that very little about preachers who had served the church had been included, so he did some research and added the names of all the pastors in times past, what years they had served and what important conference committees they had served on. In the eighty years of the church up until 1956, forty-two different pastors had served the church for an average of 1.9 years per pastor. Either because of the Methodist system or for some other reason, pastors don't last long at Hackleburg. Rev. Bell added to the history box pictures of former pastors, including a pretty good one of Rev. Whitko in the 1930s in a bathing suit at a church picnic. The picture was rather scandalous at the time not only because Rev. Whitko was, as someone said, "roly-poly," but more so because he showed up without a top on his bathing suit.

So the official history of the Hackleburg church varies little from the official church histories of many small town churches (or big churches or country churches for that matter). The only problem is these "histories," which tend to feature who the trustees were, when the buildings were erected and when the women's organizations were formed (and reformed and reorganized and merged), don't really tell us much of the church as a living organism with its own personality. There is not much about the heroic moments as well as the faltering moments.

The real stories of churches should be told as a continuation of the book of Acts. They are the stories of God working out his purposes. While those purposes occasionally include such dramatic developments as dreams, visions and miracles, they much more regularly involve mundane matters involving potlucks and nursery classes and tenors in the choir and little short pews. More important, God uses the quirks and the idiosyncrasies of ordinary people who are saved by grace to do great things.

It is conceivable that in heaven a lot of stories will be told and retold, and we will marvel at how insignificant events were actually part of God's greater plan. We will also marvel at how events quickly forgotten actually redirected the big story in significant ways.

And so we share just a very few of the stories of Hackleburg, as they were told at the time they actually took place. As with all family stories, they are meant to be told at family gatherings, such as men's meetings or Sunday school class gatherings or whenever people need something quick because they forgot they were to lead in "devotions." The big story is not yet complete, of course. When Christ comes to take his Bride, that is, the Church—and that includes Hackleburg—we will know much more.

We have been aided in telling some of these stories by Hackleburg's guardian angel, Freddy. Most churches are not aware that each has a guardian angel. It is just as well, because our religion is not a religion about angels, and we might tend to give them more credit than they deserve; and

Freddy, who is a Reluctant Angel, has really only been doing his job and seldom goes beyond the call of duty.

Even though the Triune God is not overtly mentioned much in this story, be informed that the big story is really about him and not about us.

Roll Call of the Saints of Hackleburg

Helen Dorris Hankins—Saved by grace: 1911– 1991

Marianne Dorris Johnson—Saved by grace: 1911–1983

 Lush Larkin—Saved by grace: 1862–1937

Otis Hankins—Saved by grace: 1911–1997

Marybelle Littlejohn Hasselbaum—Saved by grace: 1877–1958

Hester Holloway—Saved by grace: 1923–

Clarabell Ingram—Saved by grace: 1921–1997

Rev . Elmer Whitko—Saved by grace: 1890–1974

Harley Littlejohn—Saved by grace: 1833–1911

Bertha Winteregg Littlejohn—Saved by grace: 1847–1919

Hank Littlejohn—Saved by grace: 1836–1916

Gertrude Winteregg Littlejohn—Saved by grace: 1847–1921

Wilbur Winteregg—Saved by grace: 1880–1971

William Sprague—Saved by grace: 1871–1953

Ed Jarrett—Saved by grace: 1944–

Billy McPherson—1944–

Minnie Rittenhouse—Saved by grace: 1900–1977

Michael Anderson—Saved by grace: 1957–

CHAPTER ONE

The Methodist Revival

January 20, 1922

The revival closed at the Methodist Church Sunday night and things are quiet in Hackleburg. That is unfortunate. As Freddy, the Reluctant Angel, points out, things are not supposed to be quiet in Hackleburg following a Methodist revival. The farmers who drink coffee down at Lush's City Café shouldn't be there. They should be home, peeking cautiously out of their windows, on the lookout for zealous Methodists wanting to talk to them about their souls. The City Café crowd used to lose one or two to the Methodists every year. Farmers would come to town unsuspecting, stop to get coffee, and before they knew it they were down at the revival meeting confessing their sins.

And they weren't alone. A lot of Hackleburg would be with them. The Methodist revival was usually the most excitement Hackleburg saw all year: revival preachers from

17

exotic, far-off places—like Ohio . . . old men shouting "Hallelujah" and sometimes jumping over pews . . . young girls getting saved and sanctified and confessing sins that a lot of people were interested in hearing about. When the revival got a full head of steam, Aunt Bertha Healy would swoon and faint dead away. And as sure as not, Bill Hollyfield would get saved. Every year Bill got saved. No evangelist was ever a failure with old Bill in the crowd. During the year he always backslid enough so he needed to get saved all over again, sometimes several times during the same revival.

And when the revival was past people would walk down Main Street singing songs like "Love Lifted Me" and "Higher Ground," and the women in Erma's Beauty Shop would talk about who got saved and what sins got confessed and about the great sermons of the week, like the sermon on the circumcision of the heart and the conversion of the Ethiopian eunuch. And parents of fourth graders would be explaining circumcision and what a eunuch is.

But of late, revivals have come and gone without much of a stir. That is fine with Pastor Hippenstein. The pastor can't take too much excitement. He's not comfortable when people jump over pews or faint or start talking about marching to close up the pool hall. Last year they talked that way and he didn't sleep for two nights, worried that they were serious and they would want him to lead the parade. The pastor confided to his wife, Erma, that the crowds weren't bad this year and the offering was acceptable. Evangelist Billy Satler was properly restrained. He mentioned hell once or twice to keep the old-timers happy, but his hell wasn't so hot that the respectable Methodists got uncomfortable. Methodists are coming up in the world, you know. They are teachers and businessmen and leading citizens and their "Amens" are spoken with softer voices. In a few years they'll probably speak them silently and in a few more years after that they'll probably speak them not at all.

For some people what went on at the Methodist Church last week shouldn't even be called revival. The meetings were more like polite social gatherings. Marybelle Hasselbaum will tell you that. She likes to talk about the real Hackleburg revivals—about the year the evangelist was Wilbur "Hot Lips" Heaton, a black man who once played in a jazz band in New Orleans. The young people came and followed Wilbur in a big procession when he walked around the church playing his trumpet. On the fourth night he led the whole procession down the center aisle to the altar. Twenty-three kids got saved that night. Or the year they had Hattie Broadman, who wore hats and preached in a different hat every night. Or the year the Methodists charged out of church and down the street and closed down Lush Larkin's West Side Saloon. It took him all of three months to get himself organized so he could open again as Lush's Downtown Saloon on Main Street.

Almost all the Methodists date their conversion to one of the revivals—Alfred Brackley, Jessica Conwell, or William Goins, the banker. And Marybelle will tell you of her own conversion, fairly dramatic the way she tells it: She was sinking deep in sin, far from the peaceful shore, very deeply stained within, sinking to rise no more. She was in rebellion, in deep need of Jesus, despite her godly parents, with a heavy burden of guilt, but Jesus reached down and took her by the hand—glory be—and gave her peace and anointed her with the Holy Ghost. She was age four at the time.

But most of all Marybelle will tell you about the big one, the first revival, back in the winter of 1878, the revival that changed the town, closed down the saloons and launched the gospel movement in Hackleburg, the revival where her daddy, her dear departed daddy, was converted.

That was the year they had the woman trance evangelist, Mrs. L. L. Persimmon, Sister Persimmon (L. L. stood for Lena Leone). She came to town to hold union meetings down in the old Grange Hall at the end of Main Street. Union meetings were where everyone got together, all the churches and all the people, to cooperate. Of course there was only one church, and not too many people to cooperate, even if they wanted to. Hackleburg was in a godless state at the time with only the Baptists to present a gospel witness, and the Baptists were so full of immersion, predestination, imputed righteousness and eternal security that they were no match for the devil and his angels. Rowdies shot off guns on Main Street. There was no temperance witness. There was cursing on every street corner. And the saloons outnumbered the churches four to one.

But, as Marybelle told it, Sister Persimmon preached and the Holy Ghost came, and Marybelle's daddy, Harley Littlejohn, who had not had the privilege of hearing the gospel, was gloriously saved, as well as her mother, Bertha Littlejohn—she was a Winteregg you know, and her aunt Gertrude Littlejohn, she was a Winteregg too, and her uncle Harvey Littlejohn—all gloriously saved, and the revival broke and continued for weeks, into March, until they finally had to quit so the farmers could plant their crops. Those who were converted studied the Scriptures and were convinced of the Methodist way and so they called in the presiding elder and organized the Hackleburg Methodist Episcopal Church, and her daddy was the first Sunday school superintendent and her mother, her dear sainted mother, organized the Women's Christian Temperance Union and became its first president. Hackleburg has been a beacon in the dark world ever since.

Now according to Freddy, the Reluctant Angel who was a key player in the actual event, there is more to the story. Not to take anything away from Marybelle; she has a sanctified heart, but Marybelle was an infant in 1878 and Freddy has been around a long time.

In Freddy's version, if guns were shot off on Main Street, there was cursing on every corner and saloons outnumbered churches four to one, it was mostly because of Marybelle's own daddy. Harley Littlejohn was a scoundrel, a despicable scoundrel, along with his brother, Harvey Littlejohn. Together they set the standard for despicable scoundrelhood, not only in Hackleburg, but in all of Pike County. They lived, two old bachelors, down in the old Greeley place on the east side of town. Indeed they *were* the east side of town. Everyone else lived on the north side, or south or west, just as far from the Littlejohns as they could get.

The Littlejohn boys between them owned twenty-one coon dogs, about thirteen old sows, a couple of boars, along with the little pigs belonging to the sows or who knows who, some chickens, an old horse and a milk cow, five shotguns, barrels of homemade whiskey, and collections of old buggy parts and outhouses. All in their natural habitat, which included weeds and stray cats and bugs and who knows what.

It was a one-property slum. The Littlejohn boys never took baths, never shaved and they cursed a lot. They cursed in the morning and they cursed at night, and most of the time in-between. They cursed in soft voices and in loud voices. They cursed the coon dogs, the pigs, the chickens, each other, the Baptists and the little kids who would wander curiously down to the east side of town to get a peek. The Littlejohn boys drank their whiskey and shot off their guns, Civil War Springfield musket rifles. And when the wind was in the right direction, or, actually in any direction, but especially when it was from the east, the smell of the pigs and the outhouses and barking of the dogs and the loud cursing voices would waft over the little community, and Hackleburg seemed like the town that God had forgotten.

This was especially for the Winteregg sisters, Bertha and Gertrude, on the far west side of town, who saw themselves as the last hope for decency and culture and respectability in Hackleburg. Bertha and Gertrude read Elizabeth Barrett

Browning, Louisa May Alcott and T. S. Eliot and dreamed of far-off places like Paris or London or New York, or at least Pikeville, the county seat. They were teachers. Actually, they were half of the whole teaching staff at the Hackleburg school, such as it was, Hackleburg not being much for education. They tried to start a literary society and a music society and a reading club in Hackleburg, but every effort failed. The town was hopelessly backward. It didn't even have a Methodist Church.

But the Winteregg twins never stopped dreaming, for Hackleburg or for themselves. Someday some knight in shining armor would come to sweep them off their feet, which would have taken some doing, for both had passed well beyond the 200-pound mark and were approaching 250, if not 275. But if there were no knight in shining armor, at least perhaps they could meet someone in town who had read a book, seen a play or visited somewhere in the world beyond Pikeville.

The Winteregg twins, therefore, became the logical hostesses for Sister L. L. Persimmon when she came to town to hold the Union Mission. Lena Leone (that's where the L. L. came from), had asked the Lord to show her a spot that needed a miracle, and she closed her eyes and put her finger on the map, and it landed right on the H of Hackleburg. And so she packed her bags and came by train. When she arrived she asked the station master where she should preach and where she should stay and he suggested the Grange Hall and the Winteregg sisters and within two days she was in business.

She wore a long, flowing robe and preached each night for an hour and forty minutes about how God had sent her and God was a God of miracles and the saints should pray. Pray the desires of their hearts. Pray to God for the unexpected. Pray for revival. The saints, such as they were, did their best. Bertha and Gertrude for example, hadn't been to church for several years, but the revival, if that's what you called it, was at least something different in town, something to break the monotony and offer hope. But other than the sisters, the Baptist preacher, Ezra Cummins, who up to this time had had a monopoly on religion in Hackleburg, and one or two others, there were no takers for revival. For the first week of preaching there were no miracles, no conversions and very few people in attendance.

It was during that revival week that Harley and Harvey Littlejohn went on one of their coon hunting/drinking/cursing sprees. That was when they would put twenty-one coon dogs in a woods and let them loose. Most of the coons in Hackleburg township knew about these sprees and cleared out while the clearing out was good. They would leave town, that is, the woods, and take a little vacation for several days over in the next township. Not that Harley and Harvey could ever hit any of the coons with a Civil War Springfield musket rifle when they were drunk, but it is stressful as a coon to have twenty-one yapping dogs disturbing the woods accompanied by two trigger-happy drunken hunters. The dogs would have a good time. They would sniff and run and bark just like they knew what they were doing and finally pick a tree to stand around and Harley and Harvey would fire twenty or twenty-five shells with their Civil War Springfield musket rifles and blow the tops out of the tree, trying to hit a coon that wasn't there, and enjoying a swig or two between each shot. When the bottle was empty they would go home and the dogs would follow and the coons would return home from vacation and everyone would be happy.

Except on this night, January 30, 1878. It had been a fairly mild winter, but a cold spell had come. The temperature was around zero and the wind was blowing. Harley and Harvey had had their good time shooting up the woods and drinking whiskey and were on their way home when Harley decided on a shortcut across the

Henderson pond. On his way across the pond the ice broke and Harley, totally soused, fell in. And he began to thrash around. He called out for Harvey and for his coon dogs but they had gone another way. When calling didn't work he tried cursing. He cursed his brother and every one of his coon dogs by name.

When cursing didn't help, he tried praying. "God help me. God, I ain't been so good but help me." Then he started to bargain: "Tell you what. You get me out of here and I'll go to church, to that blankety-blank Baptist Church . . ." At that point he went under, and then up. "Excuse me, God, I didn't mean to says blankety-blank. Tell you what, God, I'll get rid of my pigs. I'll get rid of my blankety-blank coon dogs." Down he went under the water again. When he came back he said, "Excuse me, God, I didn't mean to says blankety-blank. God, I'll even get rid of my whiskey."

When he got to the whiskey part, the Heavenly Father told Freddy to swing into action. Freddy's line was, "Fear not"—that's what angels always say—"Fear not, the Lord is with you," which he proclaimed in his best angel voice. Which Harley heard. For Harley really had a hole in his heart where God belonged. "'Fear not'? God, I'm drowning. It's not a time for 'fear not.' Get me out of here and then I'll think of 'fearing not.'"

The Lord let him down one more time and then gave Freddy the word, and Freddy in his stern angel voice said, "Harley, you ox head." (The ox head part was not from the Heavenly Father; Freddy added that on his own.) "Put your feet down. It is only four feet deep." Sure enough, it was only three feet, ten inches deep. Harley's foot rested on solid ground, and Harley tried to remember what it was he had said to God when he was not in his right mind. And Freddy said, "Too late, Harley, you already promised."

And so Harley got out of the pond, but he was still in trouble. Now instead of drowning he was going to freeze to death. He was one big hunk of ice, like a frozen statue. People would look out over the field and think it was a tree stump, and they wouldn't find him until spring. So Harley got humble again. "God, I've got to get to a house. God, you get me to a house and I'll clean up. I'll take a bath. I'll get respectable. I'll get married. Whatever." It was a mile from town, and his beard and his clothes were caking up with ice and he was beginning to feel numb, like maybe he just wanted to lie down and go to sleep. And now Freddy had one of the biggest jobs of his angel life. "Walk, Harley. Walk. Fear not. Fear not, Harley, the Lord is with you. Do you believe, Harley, do you believe? The Lord is with you." The whiskey worked like antifreeze in his veins and Harley walked and he staggered and he walked. Then he saw a light, a house. "Walk, Harley, walk. Fear not, the Lord is with you. Just make it to the house, Harley."

Ahead, where the light was, Sister L. L. Persimmon, the trance evangelist, in the home of Bertha and Gertrude, there in the middle of the night, had gone into one of her trances. In her trance she had a vision of the Bible story of the maniac of Gadara and the man from whom Jesus drove the demons, which went into the pigs, who disappeared into the water. Only in her vision there was this strange part about coons coming into the woods and saying good-bye to the coon dogs who would never more return because the coon dogs were going to be going to a far country. And she prayed, "Lord, I am willing to drive out the demons, but I don't know any maniacs of Gadara, or any coon dogs. You'll just have to send them my way."

And Bertha Winteregg, for her part, was also praying. Sister Persimmon had said, "Pray for a miracle." Bertha had prayed for miracles in general but Sister Persimmon had said, "Pray for a specific miracle. What is the deepest desire of your heart? Faith can move mountains." Now, Bertha had a mountain and she had a deep desire. So she took a deep breath and let it out. "God, I need a husband. I'm not too choosy. I know I can't be, under the circumstances. And I don't know where to go to find one." Then in a step of great faith she said, "God, you'll have to send him here." Then she took an even bigger step of faith. "God, I mean right now, right this instant."

That's when they heard the thud. Bertha and Gertrude and Sister Persimmon, coming of her trance, heard the thud on the front porch. They ran to the door, and then let out a shriek. It was the abominable snow man, a monster encased in ice, unconscious. They dragged him in and laid him on the floor next to the fire. And they pulled off the dirty, frozen clothes and rubbed his skin, and washed him up and put one of Sister Persimmon's white robes on him, which was all they had for clothes. And then they lifted him into a clean bed. Sister Persimmon, who never doubted her visions, said, "Thank you, Lord, for the maniac." And Bertha, stunned, kept saying to herself, "It's Harley. Harley. God sent me Harley. Well, I said I couldn't be choosy, and it is a man. I know that now for sure." She had just undressed him. And all stretched out, in a white robe, smelling of perfumed soap and with pink skin, he didn't look bad at all.

Finally, Harley opened his eyes. He smelled the perfume, saw he was in a white robe, looked at his pink skin and felt the warm bed, so he thanked God that as long as he had to die he had made it to heaven. There was even the smell of beef stew cooking on the stove. He tried to make his eyes focus on what appeared to be three beautiful angels. They must have been the ones who spoke to him. Why had they called him ox-head? He wasn't an ox-head. Freddy, the Reluctant Angel, rolled his eyes.

Sister Persimmon began to pray. She prayed for the soul of this poor maniac from Gadara and went on about pigs and demons and the waters of the sea and the blood of Jesus and coon dogs and the prodigal son who had strayed to a far country. Then she took up with Abraham who left the far country to go to a new land, and how God promised him he would be the father of a great nation. Somewhere between the maniac of Gadara and the prodigal son and Abraham, Harley got a good old-fashioned Methodist infilling, though at the time he thought it was a Baptist infilling. When Bertha heard the part about the father of a great nation, she reasoned that if Harley would be the father of a great nation, he would have to have a wife to be the mother, and she took his hand and sighed deeply.

A lot happened during the next four days in Hackleburg. Miracle #1: For starters, Bertha, Gertrude and Sister Persimmon together began their clean-up of the Littlejohn one-property slum. They burned outhouses and buggy parts and washed, purged and used up all the lye soap in Hackleburg. Harvey, Harley's brother, mean old coon-hunting, whiskey-drinking bachelor that he was, stood with his mouth open in stunned disbelief all four days. He outdid some of Sister Persimmon's trances. Nobody, especially no woman, had been in that house for months, maybe years. And nobody, especially no woman, had ever said to him with authority he could not refuse, as Sister Persimmon did, "Harvey, take off your clothes, you're gettin' a bath." And, for that matter, nobody, man or woman, had cooked up beef stew like Bertha Winteregg did, just for him, or had ever brought him a new shirt and pants from town.

That was one thing that happened. There was more. Miracle #2: Harley and Harvey's pigs ran away. They just disappeared. It was rumored that after Sister Persimmon had turned over the whiskey barrels the pigs had helped themselves and were well fortified for their journey. It was also rumored they ended up at Stan Henry's farm down the road. As far as Sister Persimmon was concerned, however, they had disappeared into the sea.

Miracle #3: Harley took his coon dogs down to the saloon and gave them all away, with only this stipulation: If you got a coon dog, you needed to come to one of Sister Persimmon's meetings at the Grange Hall.

Miracle #4:. Most of Hackleburg showed up at the Grange Hall. The big attraction was Harley and Harvey, clothed and in their right minds. Harley gave a revised version of the events that led to his conversion, but it was enough to soften the hearts of some of the most hardened sinners in Hackleburg. Sister Persimmon didn't let a single one of those hardened sinners with softened hearts get away.

Miracle #5: A Methodist Church got started. Now they might have all become Baptists, but brother Ezra Cummins, the Baptist minister, made a bad mistake. He was ready to take credit for all the conversions. His faithful preaching and prayers had finally borne fruit. Then he made a comment about how this revival was preordained in God's great plan— God knew that Harley, Harvey, the Winteregg twins and all the others would believe, and how they would all be baptized in the Henderson pond, even if they had to break the ice. They would be baptized three times backwards. And Harley Littlejohn at that very instant became convinced of the truth of the Methodist way.

That mention of immersion three times backwards in the Henderson pond launched the Methodist Church. Harvey had been already immersed, not three times but three times three times three, forward and backward and sideways. As a result, he felt a tug toward baptism by sprinkling in a warm building. Even though he didn't know much about Methodism, he spoke with great fervor about the superiority of the Methodist way so that most of the converts ended up being Methodist instead of Baptist. They called the Methodist circuit-riding preacher, young Davie Gage, to come and preach the gospel and include them on the circuit. So Davie came, and when he made his report at the conference about the revival at Hackleburg, the town that everyone thought God had forgotten, all the preachers cheered. And Davie Gage got an advancement at the next annual conference.

Miracle #6: Harley and Bertha got married three weeks later in the Grange Hall. Sister Persimmon came back to do the wedding. Most of the town showed up. When they saw Harley in a suit and a tie, shaven and respectable, and the beaming Bertha at his side, they believed. Miracles happen. Three weeks after that Harvey and Gertrude were married. Harvey never really courted and never really proposed, which was fine because Harvey was shy. He had no idea how to court or how to propose. He liked God's way. God just tells you who to marry and you do it.

Miracle #7: Hackleburg Methodist Episcopal Church would make sure, at least for the next forty years or so, that there would be a yearly revival, anointed by God, bathed with prayer and attended by angels, including Freddy who always had to show up.

Well, Harley and Bertha and Harvey and Gertrude are all gone now. But they've got children scattered here and there who still support the revival. Like Marybelle, her brother Wilbur and her cousin Hank. Revival is in their genes. They grew up with it. But the revivals are tamer. Not so much dancing in the aisles or waving the handkerchiefs or jumping over pews. But that's all right, the Heavenly Father assures Freddy. The church will go on, and God will find a way.

CHAPTER TWO

Susanna Wesley—
Methodist Dog

July 1, 1924

B rother Benny, that is Rev. Benjamin Wooley, is off to
a good start as pastor of the Hackleburg church.
Brother Benny was appointed at the annual conference to Hackleburg. He's been on the job only about three
weeks, but he is feeling much better about the appointment,
and himself. This is good, because Brother Benny had some
problems at his last appointment over at the Bartlesville
Circuit, mostly at the Pleasantview Church where, I guess
because he is young and without a lot of experience, he alien-
ated the Ladies' Aid Society and Bertha Logan—she is the
president—and the trustees, and about everybody else in
the church—and he was only trying to be helpful. They don't
teach you some things when you are training to be a minister, like never, never interfere with the Ladies' Aid Society,
even if you are trying to be helpful.

It seems the women of the Ladies' Aid Society wanted new indoor toilets, and the trustees, some of whom are husbands of the women in the Ladies' Aid Society, didn't think they needed indoor toilets. The old privy had served the church well for the past twenty-eight years and still had a lot of life in it. Furthermore, the church needed a new roof.

Now an experienced pastor knows that at a time like that one ought to retreat to his study and read the book of Ecclesiastes. Not Pastor Wooley. He was going to solve the problem. Patch the roof and upgrade the privies. Put privies on cement foundations and put lids on the seats. Maybe add a privy, so you have "Men" and "Women." That wasn't what the Ladies' Aid women wanted nor what the trustees wanted. In fact it was just about the dumbest idea anyone had heard of, and it wasn't long before both men and women noticed things about Brother Benny they didn't like. His pants were too short and when he preached his socks sagged and this annoyed people. And he blew his nose too loudly into his handkerchief, and as the annual conference approached the people thought maybe they needed a new pastor, and that's how Brother Benny got to Hackleburg. He came in with humility and with a new life Bible verse, Proverbs 10:14: "Wise men lay up knowledge but the babbling of a fool brings ruin near."

His Bible verse got tested the very first week, not by a Bertha Logan, but by a future Bertha, Helen. Helen Dorris. Helen was thirteen years old and was obviously not overawed by God nor man. Brother Benny sensed from his very first encounter with Helen that this young woman might some day not only run the Ladies' Aid Society, she could be the district president—or be a traveling evangelist or run a missions hospital in some far-off country.

"Brother Benny, " she announced a week ago last Tuesday in the parsonage living room. Brother Benny was on a step ladder hanging pictures. She startled him—he about fell off the ladder. He didn't know she was there. Of course she didn't knock. She never did. She lived right across the street from the parsonage, and she thought the parsonage was just an extension of her own home.

"Brother Benny"? He was sort of hoping he might be "Rev. Wooley" in this new church. He had always wanted to be "Reverend," but pastors aren't "Reverend" at Hackleburg; they are "Brother," even to little kids.

"Will you do Susanna's funeral for us?"

Brother Benny was not aware anybody had died. "Susanna who?" he asked.

"Susanna Wesley. You know, mother of the Methodists. We're responsible for her funeral and we wanted you to give the sermon."

There must be some logical explanation, but Brother Benny couldn't figure what it was.

"We?"

"My sister Marianne and I and Otis, along with Lush."

"When is this funeral?"

"We think Thursday or Friday, whenever Susanna gets back from Pikeville."

Brother Benny got down from the ladder. They had a perfectly good funeral home in Hackleburg.

"Why is she at Pikeville?" This was a cautious question.

Helen sounded exasperated. Preachers can be so, so backward.

"Because that's the only place they stuff them. She's at the taxidermist."

For some reason, it must have been the Holy Spirit, Brother Benny remembered his Bible verse, "The babbling of a fool brings ruin near." There were a lot of things he might have said at that moment, some of which would have spoiled his whole ministry there and even in the future, such as thirty years from now when Helen would likely be district president of the Ladies' Aid Society.

So he was wise. "Tell me about Susanna."

"She is the Methodist dog. She's been baptized. Marianne and Otis and I baptized her. And she attends church every Sunday. And Lush has agreed to have her stuffed, so she can always be with us."

Suddenly Helen's face fell. "Oh dear," she said as something new occurred to her. "How can we bury her if she's stuffed? You can't have a funeral without a burial."

Brother Benny remembered his verse, "The babbling of a fool brings ruin near." He thought of a wise thing: "We'll bury her heart. They don't stuff the real heart."

That did it. He had shown great wisdom. Helen was overjoyed. Brother Benny had a new fan.

"A good idea," she exclaimed. "We'll bury her heart, and dedicate the rest of her."

Dedicate? Brother Benny winced.

Well anyway, the funeral came off. It took place on Monday. It took them a little while to do the stuffing. The Sunday before the funeral the junior high Sunday school class had the biggest attendance they had had for five years— twelve kids. They discussed, debated actually, whether dogs go to people heaven or to animal heaven. Helen and Marianne, the twins, argued that while most animals go to animal heaven, Susanna was different. She belonged in a people world. Furthermore, she had been baptized and came to church every week.

Monday turned out to be a beautiful day, and a good crowd gathered in Lush's hollyhock garden. Brother Benny was surprised by the crowd, it being a dog funeral and all. Lush Larkin, rightful owner of Susanna, showed up in a suit, which, since he hardly ever wore a suit, indicated this was a most special occasion. And Marybelle Hasselbaum, president of the Ladies' Aid, as well as the WCTU (Women's Christian Temperance Union), not only came but sang a song, "When They Ring Them Golden Bells." Some other kids and their parents were there and Susanna herself, that is, the stuffed version. They placed her on a little stand, and she looked as though she wanted to wag her tail and join in, and maybe sing a song. And everybody shed a tear or two, especially Lush, who shed quite a few tears. And that was very moving because no one had ever seen Lush shed a tear.

The twins, Helen and Marianne, along with Otis Hankins and the junior high class, planned to sponsor a penny supper that coming Saturday to raise money for a marker, nothing fancy, something like "Here lies Susanna Wesley, the faithful Methodist dog, 1911–1924."

Susanna did not start out to be a Methodist dog. Indeed, she was intended to be Attila the Hun, Fierce Warrior, Disrupter of Peace, whose very name would strike fear in the hearts of people, and who was specifically trained to be the haranguer of Methodists. She was the project of Lush Larkin, owner at that time of Lush's City Saloon located in the heart of downtown Hackleburg and hater of all Methodists. Lush lived next door, just to the south, of the Methodist Church, much too close in a small town like Hackleburg, where it is not good for saloon owners and Methodist churches to be side by side.

As far as the Hackleburg church was concerned, and especially Marybelle Hasselbaum, president of the Ladies' Aid Society and the WCTU, Lush's City Saloon was the corrupter of youth, a blight on the community and a cancer on the moral fabric of society. The saloon was open and rebellious sin—as opposed to secret sin, which is the most common kind in Hackleburg, like gossip, envy and pride. Open sin was like whiskey; you could see it and identify it.

Against this sin God had called Methodists to do spiritual warfare, which mostly consisted of frowning when they saw somebody even walk by Lush's Saloon. Good Methodists would cross the street and not even lend their presence to the sidewalk in front of Lush's. Spiritual warfare also consisted of gasping when they knew of men who actually went inside. Like Bob Bowen.

"Did you know Bob Bowen goes in there every Friday night?"

They also waged spiritual warfare by putting up signs on the church yard, facing toward Lush's house, with messages like "Repent," and "Mother's Sweet Prayers," right next to one that read, "Crush Lush."

The Methodists also kept their church windows to the south open during all revival meetings, so that the warnings of the evangelist, about hell and fire and judgment upon all who sell the devil's drink, could waft across those few yards between the church and Lush's house and find their way into Lush's open windows, so he would know how much they cared for him. And on Temperance Sundays, which were in Hackleburg about once a month, even when it was cold, they would open the windows and belt out "My Mother's Tears Will Follow Me," and "Do You Slumber in Your Tent, Christian Soldier?" so loudly it could be heard all the way downtown.

And the Methodists were successful, not in closing down the saloon but in loading so much guilt on the men who patronized Lush's that the men no longer felt comfortable entering the saloon by the front door. They would park their buggies and their Model T's over by Haskin's Lumber Company, a block away, and sneak down the alley and enter by the rear door, so no Methodist would see them.

In retaliation Lush waged warfare in his own way. He railed in the saloon, in the barber shop and in the meat market about the hypocrisy of the Methodists, who preached against drinking but who were gluttons at their potlucks and were addicted to coffee. On Sunday mornings he would get out his sprinkling can to water his hollyhocks and would "accidentally" water the seats of the churchgoers' buggies and Model T's that were parked anywhere near his property.

But his biggest weapon was chicken feathers, which he burned. And not just chicken feathers, sometimes chicken heads, chicken feet and anything dead, but mostly chicken feathers. Bags of feathers, from his chicken coop and all the coops he could find. He offered free drinks at the saloon for bags of chicken feathers so that he could burn them on Sunday mornings in his trash barrel when the Methodist windows were open and the wind was from the west. Even when the wind wasn't from the west he hooked up his newfangled electrical fan to blow the smell through the Methodist windows.

And the Methodists would choke and cough, suffering for the sake of righteousness, and speak Methodist cuss words like "darn" and "O dear" and "heavens to Betsy" and "fizzle-fazzle," and would intone with heartfelt emotion the Psalms: "Do we not hate them that hate thee, O God, and do we not loathe them that rise up against thee? We hate them with perfect hatred." There is nothing like burning chicken feathers to test the sanctification of Methodists.

But even that wasn't enough. Lush had another weapon in his battle against self-righteousness—his dog Buster. His slow-learning dog Buster, whose goal in life was to be a real live hunting coon dog and who was training for his big chance by chasing squirrels, running them up trees and barking at them triumphantly, like a real coon dog treeing coons. There was hardly a squirrel in all Hackleburg that Buster had not treed—including Frisky, who was actually a stuffed squirrel, a big, fat, stuffed fox squirrel with his tongue permanently stuck out. On Sunday mornings, Sunday nights and prayer meeting nights, Lush would put Frisky the stuffed squirrel on the bottom branch of the silver maple, closest to the Methodist's open window, with its tongue stuck out, mocking that dog, and Buster would bark and bark and bark, and the Methodists couldn't do anything but close their windows and say their Methodist cuss words like "fizzle-fazzle," and "darn," and intone their Psalms, "Do we not hate them that hate thee, O God?"

Then one day Buster got run over by an automobile. He was the first traffic fatality in all of Hackleburg township. It so happened it was Marybelle Hasselbaum, president of the Women's Christian Temperance Union (WCTU) and the Methodist Ladies' Aid, in her new Model T, who was just learning to drive, who ran over Buster. In the mind of Lush Larkin that was dirty fighting. That was the last straw. Bad enough the Methodists put up their signs and sang their temperance songs, but to run over an innocent dog, a helpless slow-learning dog at that, to open the throttle on that Model T and rev that machine up to who knows how fast (maybe twenty miles per hour!) and murder a dog—that was a new low in the atrocities of war.

It must be said that the women of the WCTU did not totally disbelieve the running-down-the-dog charge. Marybelle was known as a courageous woman, and maybe she did open that throttle to do the dog in, but if so, it was only for the cause of righteousness.

The truth is that Buster, slow-learning dog that he was, had thought the Model T was a coon, a real live coon. He had never seen a coon before, and he was supposed to be a coon-hunting dog, and the vehicle was going so slowly (closer to five miles an hour than twenty) that he took it on, and lost.

Lush vowed revenge. A bigger, badder and uglier dog—a pit bull, a Doberman pinscher, a German shepherd or a Siberian husky—one that not only would bark, but would snarl and chase the kids from the youth group when their ball rolled into his hollyhock garden. That's when he heard men talking at the saloon about a dog out at Henry Tenant's farm that Henry was trying to get rid of because she howled like a wolf at the moon, at the cows, at the chickens and the pigs, and was disrupting life in the Tenants' barnyard. The cows weren't giving as much milk and the chickens weren't laying as many eggs.

Lush heard the words "wolf," "howl" and "disrupt" and in his mind he pictured a ferocious wolf out on the prairie, teeth bared, head of the wolf pack, striking fear into the hearts of buffalo and moose and grizzly bears—no rabbits for him, just big stuff. And he could see in his mind this wolf after each successful hunt, standing tall over his fallen foe, letting out his bloodcurdling howl, and Lush said to himself, "That's the dog I want."

So he went out to the Tenant farm and claimed the dog for five dollars. He was a bit disappointed at the dog's appearance. Instead of looking like a wolf she resembled an overgrown beagle. He was further displeased by her tail, which kept wagging. He was not sure vicious dogs wagged their tails that much. But she could howl, and she did so for him, as if on cue, right there in the barnyard, a long, mournful howl. If you used your imagination you could call it "bloodcurdling," so he brought the dog home.

Lush named her Attila the Hun, the Worker of Havoc, whose name stands for Destruction. He started to train her to howl on cue. He had one religious record for his Victrola, a record his mother had given him, of Sister Bertha Smalley singing, "When They Ring Them Golden Bells," and he played it over and over. He coaxed and cajoled Attila the Hun until every time she heard organ music, and especially the song "When They Ring Them Golden Bells," she would howl.

A couple of Sundays later, Attila the Hun had her chance. It was a warm summer day. The Methodist windows were open. But even better, Lush's arch enemy, Marybelle Hasselbaum, was singing that very song, "When They Ring Them Golden Bells" as a solo. It was a favorite song of Marybelle's and she was dedicating it to the memory of her dear departed Great-Aunt Mary who had heard those bells and had gone to heaven. That is, she had died only the week before.

And in the middle of verse two, while Marybelle sang the words, "Don't you hear the bells a' ringin', don't you hear the angels singin'?" Attila the Hun, stationed under the Methodist window, launched into the most intense, mournful, sustained howl that any dog was capable of, in the key of A flat.

At this point there were a number of different reactions inside the church. Marybelle herself, caught up in the music and the tenderness of the message, with thoughts of Great-Aunt Mary and heaven and golden streets, her hands clasped over her bosom and her eyes closed, was convinced the angels were actually singing. It wasn't a sound like she thought angels would make, but who was she to question how angels sound. They were right there at her side. She couldn't see them, but the sound was there. So she continued singing, with the angels.

Margaret Hanfield, over on the organ, was sure the organ was breaking down. The stops had gone berserk. Organs have feelings, too, and this organ had suffered for years at Hackleburg, and it had had enough, and was rebelling, in the key of A flat. Margaret pounded that keyboard, trying to get the organ under control. She went up the scale and down, which lent more sound effects and doubly convinced Marybelle that the angels really were singing. Maybe this was the time of the end. Perhaps this was the Rapture, the time of the Lord's return.

Harry Bloomfield, fire chief, thought lightning had struck the town's fire siren, setting it off, haywire, and it was probably ready to explode and would take the whole town with it, and he got up and ran from the church. The widow ladies in the fifth and sixth rows on the left side thought that Marybelle herself had supplied the sound, to give drama to the music. Marybelle was their Gideon, head of the WCTU, and she had circled Jericho six times and this was the seventh, the trumpets were sounding and Jericho's walls were tumbling down. It was an act of God, and they clasped their hands over their bosoms and thought beautiful thoughts.

Helen and Marianne Dorris, the twins, age six, looked at each other and said, "It is a dog, a dog that howls." In God's mysterious ways, just as he sent a donkey to carry Mary and Joseph to Bethlehem and a dove to Noah after the flood, so God had sent a dog to Hackleburg. When the service was over, and it was over pretty quickly, Helen and Marianne were the first ones out the door. And they were right. It was a dog. A big, lovable overgrown beagle with a tail wagging twenty-five miles a minute. They hugged that dog, and then the tail wagged fifty miles a minute. Helen said, "O dog, you came to sing with us. Do you know Jesus, too?" The rest of the congregation, the widow ladies and the old men and the kids and Harry Bloomfield and Margaret Hanfield and Marybelle Hasselbaum, came out and said, "Well, I'll be. It was a dog making that noise. I wonder whose dog it is."

Over next door Lush Larkin was peeking out behind the curtains. He didn't know how to react. He was pleased he had trained his dog so well. She howled on cue just as he taught her. But the Methodists weren't cooperating. They were supposed to be angry and frustrated and muttering Methodist cuss words like "heavens to Betsy" and "fizzle-fazzle," and slamming the windows down and reading angry, vindictive psalms. They were not supposed to be coming out and saying, "Well, I'll be. It was a dog."

That afternoon Helen and Marianne Dorris, age six, went over to Lush Larkins' house. They had always been afraid to go over there before. Lush Larkin was mean and said naughty words and yelled at all kids. But maybe Lush Larkin was not so bad if he owned such a friendly dog. They hugged and petted that dog and asked Mr. Larkin where he got it, and was it a boy or a girl, and what was its name. When he said, "Attila the Hun," they said they had never heard of such a silly name and asked whether that was a boy's name or a girl's name. When he said it was a boy's name, Helen said, "Mr. Larkin, this is a girl dog and it should not have a boy's name." Would it be all right, they wondered, if they gave it a girl's name and how about Susanna Wesley because they had heard about Susanna Wesley in Sunday school and she was a Methodist.

Before he knew it, Lush Larkin, who had never encountered such talkative and aggressively friendly females before, especially females age six, and had never heard of the mother of Methodism, agreed to rename his dog Susanna Wesley.

The next Sunday Susanna was back under the windows, and she howled again when the music was played. Only people didn't call it a howl. It was more like a third alto part beefing up the choir in the key of A flat. It was not as though the dog was disrupting the music, it was more like she was joining the music. And when the people came out of church and Helen Dorris told them the dog's name was Susanna Wesley because she was a Methodist dog, they petted the dog on the head and said, "Glad to have you Susanna. Make a joyful noise unto the Lord."

When the people heard that Susanna Wesley belonged to Lush Larkin, owner of Lush's City Saloon in the heart of downtown Hackleburg, they said, "I'll be," and they felt a bit kinder toward Lush. Even Marybelle softened, despite her hidden inner pride, though she did not admit to any inner pride because she claimed to be sanctified and to be humble all the time. Marybelle's singing had drawn Susanna to Methodism, and Marybelle felt kinder toward Lush Larkin. She even said, "Hi," one day when she was driving by Lush's house in her Model T, doing eight miles an hour.

And Susanna? Well Susanna was really a sheep in wolf's

clothing. She had been born with a pure heart. She was a sanctified Methodist. She was so gentle she would not even chase squirrels. She loved children. She loved Lush. She loved Methodists. She loved the men down at Lush's City Saloon, and she didn't know anything about the bad feelings between the Methodist crowd and the saloon crowd. So during the week she sat in front of Lush's City Saloon and wagged her tail, and the men started coming in the front door of the saloon instead of the back door off the alley. On Sunday mornings, Sundays evenings and prayer meeting night and whenever they had revivals and potluck dinners Susanna would sit by the door of the Methodist Church and wag her tail and greet everyone who came. Sometimes the ones who came to the saloon were the same ones that came to the church, and Susanna Wesley never told a soul. And sometimes she sang with the music and always when the organ played "When They Ring Them Golden Bells."

When Prohibition came, and Lush's City Saloon became Lush's City Café, Methodists actually started patronizing Lush's, and the food wasn't bad. A few of the men down at the café, which used to be the saloon, visited the Methodist Church.

Helen and Marianne, who had been six, were nine and then eleven. When Susanna had two pups they asked Lush if they could have them, and they named them John and Charles Wesley, Methodist dogs, and they would bring John and Charles over to see Lush and Susanna. Sometimes they brought cookies. One day Lush asked them if just anybody could attend the Methodist Church, and Helen ran over and told Rev. Watkins. The next Sunday Lush came to church, all dressed up. People greeted him like he had been there always, as though he was part of the family, and he was really, since Susanna was part of the family and he was the owner of Susanna. And Susanna wagged her tail a hundred times a minute.

So that's why they had that funeral out in the lot behind the Hackleburg Methodist Church among the hollyhocks. And that's why Rev. Wooley talked about no member being so faithful as Susanna, and why Lush Larkin
was all dressed up in a suit and why Marybelle Hasselbaum
sang "When They Ring Them Golden Bells," and why
some of the youth will be having a bake sale to earn money
to put up a marker for "Susanna Wesley, Methodist Dog,
1911–1924."

CHAPTER THREE

The Lush Larkin Hackleburg Memorial Methodist Episcopal Glory to God Bible Wonderland Hollyhock Municipal Park

September 4, 1938

S unday is the big day! The dedication of the new Lush Larkin Hackleburg Memorial Methodist Episcopal Glory to God Bible Wonderland Hollyhock Municipal Park. They would have had the dedication back in June but the Official Board couldn't agree on what to call the park. They had formed a Naming Committee, which was a big mistake because the Naming Committee invited suggestions and people gave them—far more than what the committee wanted or needed, and with the suggestions came critiques of the suggestions other people had made.

Clarabell Ingram argued that the name had to include the word "Methodist." Bill Ingram pointed out that it was a community park and needed to have the word "Hackleburg" in it. The third and fourth grade Sunday school class, The Busy Little Hands, insisted that hollyhocks needed to be

45

included. The Naming Committee held four three-hour meetings to discuss the park name during which time three people resigned, two stormed out mad and Bill Hedge threatened to leave the church. They get passionate at Hackleburg over some things. Finally Pastor Whitley suggested they just include all the proposed names in one grand official title, and that is why it is being dedicated as the Lush Larkin Memorial Methodist Episcopal Glory to God Bible Wonderland Hollyhock Municipal Park.

And that can't hurt, in a way. Hackleburg is getting a lot of publicity from a park with a name like that. The *Pikeville Tribune* ran an article as did the *Harrisville Morning Gazette*. According to the papers, a rich millionaire gave money to the Methodist Church for this extravagant park with Bible names and it features the biggest slide in the world—well, if not in the world at least in a ten-county area and maybe in all of Indiana. People have been traveling over to Hackleburg to see it, and they are impressed. The slide is named Elijah's Chariot. It features a ladder, called Jacob's Ladder, that climbs twenty-six feet up to a platform named Mt. Nebo, which gives one a spectacular view, if not of the promised land, at least of Hackleburg. From the platform there is one slide to the north, called Babylon Slide, and one to the East, called Jerusalem Slide.

When people see it they say things like "Goodness be" and "Did ya ever see a thing like that?" The slide and the park is bringing in tourists from several counties, which is giving the local economy a boost. The ice cream business has picked up over at the City Café and the lemonade tables give it a kind of festive feel. Jenny and Margie Weaver put up the first lemonade table back in June and charged three cents a glass. Jim Larson came in two days later and advertised lemonade for two cents. Within three days there were four stands each charging one cent a glass. This is teaching the local kids a valuable lesson in economics.

Otis Hankins, trustee, confidant of Lush Larkin and generator of most of the weird ideas Hackleburg has had over the past few years, is responsible for the park. He also is taking all the criticism from the mothers of Hackleburg, plus mothers of Pikeville, and all the mothers from any-where who have come to visit. Do you know how high twenty-six feet is? And those angels climbing up and down Jacob's ladder are five years old, some of them. There is a safety hazard there, kind of a red alert, on a par with going over Niagara Falls in a barrel. And there have been some incidents. When Mary Sandburg saw her seven-year-old Joey twenty-three feet up in the air she fainted dead away and they had to have Bill Henry's ambulance come to the rescue. Bill runs the funeral home and his ambulance, which is the only one in Hackleburg, also doubles as a hearse. Sometimes Bill forgets to change the markings and while he was taking Mary Sandburg to the hospital he got a ticket for speeding to a burial.

But Otis, never at a loss to come up with an ingenious solution, simply ordered three truckloads of sawdust from the Lewis Lumber Yard. He spread the sawdust all around the slide so that so that when kids fell off they wouldn't get hurt. But all that did was create a new hazard. Kids could now climb Jacob's Ladder and either slide down the Babylonian slide or jump off into the sawdust like they were paratroopers in the Air Force. All the commotion created more excitement than Hackleburg had seen for years.

The slide is not the only attraction at the park. There are four horseshoe pits named after the four horsemen of the Apocalypse—the Grey, the White, the Red and the Black— and a fifth pit named after Balaam's ass, the Ass Pit. There is a merry-go-round called Elijah's whirlwind, the swings called Sweet Chariots and teeter-totters called "10726." The plaque in front of them quotes Psalm 107:26: "They mounted up to heaven, they went down to the depths." The

toilets are up-to-date one-holers with a cement base called
"Roosevelts" in honor of President Roosevelt and the contribution of the W.P.A. (Works Progress Administration).
In the center of the park is a picnic pavilion, and in the
pavilion a glass case with a stuffed dog. That would be
Susanna Wesley, Methodist Dog, 1911–1924—who some-
how figures into all of this, though most of the people have
forgotten exactly how.

The park has made Otis Hankins into a kind of local
celebrity. He is now head trustee at the church and a domi-
nant figure in the community, which seems to many people
an honor far beyond his ability and social status. Otis, the
"Old Bachelor" as he is known, is in fact only twenty-seven
years old and not from one of the respected families. But,
incredibly, he had been named executor of the Lush Larkin
estate and basically built this park, to be maintained by him
through a special fund, also part of the Lush Larkin estate,
for the "glory of God," the "encouragement of children everywhere" and the "good of the whole community."

And Otis, whom everyone has always thought of as shy
and retiring, has become, well, uppity and bullheaded. Otis
has insisted that at the dedication Brother Jesse, Sister Liza
and Lovely Daughter Zelma Humbard should lead the dedi-
catory service. However, Pastor Whitley and the Official
Board had already invited the bishop, Bishop Edgar
Hightower, for the honor. Otis was so insistent that the
Humbards be asked that the Official Board reversed itself
and Bishop Hightower was disinvited. Pastor Whitley is
mortified, betrayed by his own board. Not too many bishops once invited for a special occasion get uninvited, usurped
for some lesser—at least in the minds of Methodist offi-
cials—fly-by-night radio evangelist. Pastor Whitley is sure
this disrespect for the high office of the episcopacy will doom
his career and that he will be demoted to someplace lower
on the appointment scale. His wife, Patricia, advised him

not to worry since no church is lower on the appointment scale in the conference than Hackleburg.

Actually, to tell the truth, most folks are sort of pleased the bishop has been disinvited. No one in Hackleburg has ever seen a bishop, or scarcely know bishops even exist. When someone asked, "What is a bishop?" Clarabell Ingram described a bishop as a kind of county commissioner except with a Prince Albert long-tailed coat. Well, that sealed it. Brother Jesse was voted to be the speaker.

Brother Jesse, or at least his voice, is known by most people in Hackleburg. Brother Jesse is the radio pastor of the "Family Altar" program heard over WABC Harrisville every evening at 6:15. A lot of radios in Hackleburg pick up only one station, WABC, so there really isn't much choice if you want to listen to the radio at 6:15. Consequently, even people who otherwise have little interest in religion know about Brother Jesse and his wife, Sister Liza, and Lovely Daughter Zelma.

Brother Jesse is delighted to come and even mentioned over his program several times in the past couple of weeks about what a fine thing it is there at Hackleburg, folks building a Bible Wonderland Glory to God municipal park. Brother Jesse then told his whole radio audience how he would be going to Hackleburg to dedicate the new park for the glory of God, the encouragement of children and the good of people everywhere, and that the new municipal park is named after one of the great and generous saints of God, Lush Larkin.

That is surprising, though a lot of things have been surprising in Hackleburg lately because no one has ever quite thought of Lush Larkin as a saint, let alone a generous saint. Hadn't Lush—the old-timers remembered well—once run the Hackleburg City Saloon, which the Women's Christian Temperance Union worked for years to close down? Wasn't this the same Lush who had such a foul mouth? Not a few of the kids who grew up in Hackleburg had had their mouths washed out with soap because they repeated words they had heard while passing Lush's house. Boys from Hackleburg who joined the army in WW I knew original cuss words that even the city kids had never heard. It was almost worth an extra rank.

People shrug their shoulders over these things. The one person who might explain, Otis Hankins, the old bachelor, though he is only twenty-seven years old, doesn't talk much, and he doesn't have a wife—a lot of people who can't get information from a man can get it from his wife. All the people know is that Otis was a friend of Lush's, had been named executor of the estate, was the builder of the park and is going to be paid a salary to keep it up.

Well, there is indeed a story, and one worth telling although folks in Hackleburg aren't totally aware of it, at least not yet. It started with that dog, Susanna, the Methodist dog, and the twin girls, Helen and Marianne, who used to visit Lush and the dog, along with Otis. They were just little kids. Lush kind of took to the twins and to Otis. Lush was a bachelor and never had kids, and Otis became, well, like a son. When Lush was getting old, Otis helped him out. He mowed his lawn and looked after his barn and his hollyhocks. Sometimes Otis would come over and they would just sit in Lush's living room, the old bachelor and the young bachelor. Occasionally one would say something like, "Did you see Joe Aldridge got a new Dodge roadster?" And the other would make a grunt that sounded like "yes," and they would sit in silence and consider the significance of Joe Aldridge's roadster for the future of Hackleburg and the world.

When Lush bought his radio, they became acquainted with Brother Jesse and the Family Altar radio program at 6:15. Brother Jesse and his wife, Liza, and Lovely Daughter Zelma introduced them to a world they had known little about: the Old Testament Tabernacle, the priests and the blue garments, the ram's horn and angels. Lovely Daughter Zelma would sing songs like "Beulah Land" and "Rescue the Perishing," and occasionally Lush's favorite, "When They Ring Them Golden Bells." Lush and Otis would sit in Lush's front room and ponder these things.

In the summer of 1929, I think it was July, Lush got sick. He was really sick. As far as he was concerned, as well as Otis and the doctor, and Frank and Harry Olmstead, Lush was near death. Frank and Harry are nephews, sons of Lush's sister, Nancy. Ungrateful sons really. Scheming sons actually. They lived over in Pikeville, still do I think. They never had anything to do with Lush until they began to suspect that Lush had money and realized they were Lush's closest living relatives. And so the nephews began to get interested in Lush. They would come to visit and inquire about Lush's health and ask questions about his bank account, the value of his house and what was in his lock box.

The nephews were present the night Lush was dying. The doctor had said there was nothing more he could do for Lush. Lush had given up, nothing really to live for. His life had not been a good one. He wished it could have been different, but it was too late now. He was lying on the davenport, gasping for air and drifting in and out of consciousness. Then Lush had a vision. Bells were ringing, golden bells, and he was sliding down a big slide, a really big slide, bigger than any slide he had ever seen. At the bottom of the slide was a river, and land beyond the river, and Lush figured that would be Beulah Land or the Land of Sweet Forever. The land was filled with hollyhocks, yellow hollyhocks and purple and red and colors he had never seen before. Angels were singing about it: "There's a land beyond the river that they call the sweet forever . . . Don't you hear the bells a ringing, don't you hear the angels singing?" They were singing his song. It was so peaceful. Then the peace was disturbed by a funny little angel with red hair. The angel stood in his way and raised his hand and said, "Stop." The music stopped and Lush wasn't sliding anymore. The angel said in a stern voice, "Fear not"—angels always say "fear not"—"I have a message for you. You can't come here yet. You still have work to do."

"Work to do?" Lush was astounded. "I'm dying, in case you hadn't noticed. My work days are over."

The angel rolled his eyes, and Lush thought he heard the angel say, "You ox-head." For sure he heard the angel say, "Look around you."

Lush looked and all he saw was the slide and the hollyhocks. But there were children on the slide: Helen and Marianne, and they had cookies and they were sharing with other people. Lush knew Helen was now a missionary, way down in South America some place. Helen was sharing cookies with children who spoke a strange language.

Then the spell was broken and Lush heard voices. In the next room his nephews Frank and Harry were talking excitedly. They had been going through Lush's papers and they had found some stock certificates, 1,000 shares of Republic Steel and 2,142 shares of Pikeville Farmer's State Bank. They were celebrating. "Do you know what these are worth? We're rich. We're rich!" And Lush realized he had no will and all the stock, all his property and his house, the hollyhocks and the cookies would go to Frank and Harry, obnoxious nephews who acted just like their mother, his sister, whom he never could stand. They were going to inherit it all. They would build new homes, buy cars and spend all his money. He heard Frank say, "What will we do with the house?" "Sell it." "The hollyhocks?" "Get rid of them." "The old stuffed dog?" "Into the trash."

So Lush decided he was not about to die. He could not die. He would fight death. That little redheaded angel was right. He had work to do. And he fell into a peaceful sleep.

The next evening when Otis stopped by he found Lush sitting up. Otis looked at him strangely. Lush was supposed to be dead, or at least in the process of dying. Lush said, "In case you want to know, I am not going to die. But Otis, if I did die, what should be done with the hollyhocks?" Otis said, "We need to keep them. They're so beautiful. Everyone talks about your hollyhocks. Maybe they could be made into a park."

That night, as usual, they tuned into Brother Jesse and Sister Liza and Lovely Daughter Zelma. Brother Jesse spoke of the God of second chances, who loves us in spite of our sins and gives us a purpose in life. Lush wept and wept. Otis thought it was just part of dying, but it wasn't that at all. He was having another vision. It wasn't a red-haired angel this time, but Jesus—actually Hoffman's painting of Jesus—knocking at the door, and Lush opened the door.

Then Lush got intense. Otis had never seen him so intense. "Otis, take me to Pikeville. I have to go see James Will, my attorney. I have to have a will. You can't die without a will, you know." Lush had already decided what would be in the will. He would have his hollyhocks made into a park, and give the park to the town, no, not to the town, to the church. It would have this big slide, like the one in his vision, and the children could come, like Helen and Marianne, and he would leave enough money for someone—it had to be Otis—to care for the park.

Lush made his will. A week later (it was August of 1929) he sold all of his Republic Steel stock and all of his Pikeville Farmer's State Bank stock. He asked Otis what to do with the money. Otis said, "Put it under your mattress, I guess." So he did, a total of $95,670 in twenty-dollar gold coins. Otis had to go down into Lush's basement and put jacks under the floor to reinforce it because it was so heavy.

In a few months things started to go poorly in Hackleburg, and in a lot of places for that matter. The stock market crashed, grain prices went down, jobs dried up. People called it a Depression. In January of 1931, Republic Steel went bankrupt. In November 1933, the Farmer's State Bank of Pikeville closed. Frank and Harry saw all their riches evaporate. They weren't so interested in Lush anymore.

Meanwhile, interesting and mysterious things began happening in Hackleburg. One day there was a twenty-dollar gold piece in the church offering; it caused a great sensation. Twenty dollars is a lot of money. People wondered where it had come from. And every so often after that there would be another twenty-dollar gold piece and another after that. They would just show up, sometimes in the offering plate, sometimes in an envelope on the front seat of the preacher's car, sometimes on the preacher's desk. The twenty-dollar gold pieces brought the church through some rough times.

One evening Brother Jesse announced on the Family Altar that he would be leaving the air. Things were hard, and he couldn't pay for the air time. Lush said, "We can't let that happen," so he had Otis drive over to Harrisville to see Brother Jesse and give him a twenty-dollar gold piece and tell him there would be more from where that one came. In the fall of 1934, Helen Dorris came home from Bolivia. She's a missionary down there, you know. She came over to see Lush and brought him some cookies just like she had in the old days.

Helen went home with ten twenty-dollar gold pieces. Ten of them. It was enough to send her back to Bolivia and keep the hospital going for another whole year. Somewhere in there Lush thought he should do something for Otis, so he drove over to Harrisville, fifty miles away, and bought a brand new Deusenburg roadster. It was a beauty. Otis was flabbergasted, "Lush, I can't drive that car. What would people say. They would think I robbed a bank." So Otis never drove it. Lush put the car in the barn, way back under the old hay mow, until maybe Otis would change his mind.

And then Otis and Lush laid out the park. Bible Wonderland Glory to God Park. They picked all the names. They designed the slide, the teeter-totter, the merry-go-round and the pavilion. Lush was never happier in his life.

Lush died back in January 1937. A lot of people came to the funeral. Lush had turned out to be a pretty active Methodist the past few years. Pastor Whitley, who was new at the time and didn't know Lush in his former life, gave him a good funeral and said nice things about him, most of all that God loved him. Some people suspected but only a few knew that the twenty-dollar gold pieces had come from Lush. When the attorney informed the church about the will, that the church would get Lush's house and his barn, and there would be a fund to build and maintain the park, and Otis would be hired as caretaker, the people were astonished. And they said, "Goodness be."

And so Hackleburg has this big day Sunday. Brother Jesse and Sister Liza and Lovely Daughter Zelma will be coming to dedicate the Lush Larkin Hackleburg Memorial Methodist Episcopal Glory to God Bible Wonderland Hollyhock Municipal Park.

CHAPTER FOUR

How Hackleburg Became a Thirteen-Pie Church

December 2, 1992

H ackleburg is a thirteen-pie church. The Baptists across town are a seven-pie church—they are not very spiritual. First Church, that snobbish church located in the county seat—is only a three-pie church, and it is said that not long ago they catered in baloney sandwiches for a church meal.

A lot of people don't know about these things unless they're in touch with someone like Freddy, the Reluctant Angel. According to Freddy, being spiritual has to do with giving God your best, and the way to give God your best in Christian fellowship is with a potluck, and giving God your best at a potluck is with a pie. The more pies, the more spiritual you are. When things are going well at Hackleburg they have thirteen pies at the potlucks, but if you go to one of their potlucks and there are only eight pies, you know there is trouble some place. Families are breaking up, kids are rebelling, altos are fighting with the sopranos in the choir or preachers are without a clue, as was Rev. Howard several years ago when he announced a missionary speaker and a potluck on the opening night of the high school basketball season. They had only two pies, and it was an embarrassment to everyone.

Grandma Hester Holloway runs the Hackleburg potlucks. She is the Spiritual Advisor, Quality Control Engineer and Chief Executive Officer. It is not that she has been elected by anyone for these offices or that her name appears that way in the church directory. She has been appointed directly by God, like Melchizedek. She makes sure the chairs are set up, the tables are decorated and the is food arranged by category. She assumes responsibility for the official start of a potluck, the church version of "Gentlemen, start your engines": "Okay, preacher, you can say the prayer now." Hester also dispenses blessings. A remark like, "Why, Helen, your scalloped potatoes were wonderfully delicious tonight," confers more honor than being written up in *The Farm News*.

This is all based, of course, on biblical principles, communicated faithfully by Hester herself. She's been around long enough to have educated a couple of generations of Hackleburg cooks. Whether in Sunday school or Wednesday night Bible study, Hester preaches the Word, usually from Leviticus. People at Hackleburg don't know a lot about Romans, but they know a lot about Leviticus.

For example, when she substituted for the fifth and sixth grade Sunday School class back in October, she exhorted: "When people in Leviticus took a lamb to the temple, they took the best they had—first fruits—they didn't take a lamb with worms or dysentery or pink eye. It had to be without blemish. Now when we give something to God, like food at the church dinner, it is to be our best. You wouldn't give God something like warmed-over spinach, would you?"

Sixth-graders solemnly allowed they would not give warmed-over spinach to God, or any kind of spinach for that matter.

"God means business," Hester would say. "Ananias and Sapphira found that out when God struck them down."

Hackleburg youngsters through the years never were quite sure what Ananias and Sapphira did, but in their minds it was linked with potlucks and spinach.

Sometimes Hester taught from Matthew, especially the parable of the talents. God gives some five talents, some two talents and some one talent. We are supposed to use our talents, and Hester would relate that to food. There are five-talent cooks, two-talent cooks and one-talent cooks. When Hackleburg put out its cookbook, oh, it's been about ten years ago now, people wondered why some recipes had one star, some two stars and some five stars. That was a cross-reference to Matthew. "A five-star recipe is flagged for five-talent cooks, and should not be tried by just anybody," Hester explained. "Before you tackle a five-star recipe, like seven-layer salad, full of cream cheese, tomatoes, diced ham, taco dressing, bean sprouts and who knows what else, you might first ask God if he thinks you're ready for that." Under Grandma Hester's watchful eye, most Hackleburg cooks have risen to the level of their God-given talents. Mabel Weedman fixes homemade noodles and Tillie Tilton bakes little loaves of bread. Izzie Bellweather arranges olive slices on potato salad to form words like L-O-V-E or J-O-Y. Bachelor Harry Hilty, who if he ever had a talent had hidden it in the ground, is urged to bring potato chips. Otherwise, very little is from cans or mixes or is store-bought at a Hackleburg potluck.

Especially the five-talent pies. Elsie Goodson bakes an old-fashioned cream pie from a recipe handed down from her grandmother. Hattie Hinsford brings walnut pies made with walnuts from trees—as she explained more often than most folks want to hear—that her grandma planted as a little girl. Edna Shaftsberry brings gooseberry pie.

Waldo Carroway brings "Blue-ribbon pumpkin, just as he has every year since 1961 when Grandma Hester urged him to sign up for Baking I in 4-H. Grandma Hester herself is leader of the club. If kids in Hackleburg want to learn how to cook, Grandma Hester wants to be the one to teach them. Actually, in Hackleburg 4-H is 5-H, the Hackleburg, Happy, Hearty, Healthy Helpers. Some people say the 4-H Club is like the farm club for the Methodist potlucks. Win a ribbon at the fair for a pie and you will be asked to bring a pie to the potluck. Well, Waldo not only won the county fair but he got a blue ribbon at the state, and he has fixed the exact same pie at every potluck since then. It is the only thing he knows how to cook. Hester herself always fixes "Johnny Appleseed" apple, so named because she leaves an appleseed as a trademark in every one of her pies.

Hester is responsible for funeral dinners, too. They say down at McDiver's Funeral Home when people come in to prearrange their funerals one of the first things they ask for is for Grandma Hester to have the funeral dinner for the family. Methodists get a lot of extra funerals that way. Go out in style. Give your family the best, with one of Grandma Hester's funeral dinners.

They had a thirteen-pie potluck Sunday night at Hackleburg, at the annual Christmas potluck always held the Sunday after Thanksgiving. Everybody came, or so it seems. More people attended Sunday night for the potluck than Sunday morning for worship. Fred and Elsie Nelson, who are Baptists, were there. Fred thinks he is allowed since he was a Methodist when he was a little boy. Jean Lancaster, home from the university for Thanksgiving, was there. She wanted to see old friends and be blessed by a Hackleburg potluck before she had to go back to that university food. And old Harry was there. No one for sure knows his last name. He is the transient who shows up from time to time, and gives his story. He is either on his way from New York to Kansas to get a job, or from Kansas to New York. Sometimes he gets mixed up and doesn't remember which way he is supposed to be going. Ever since Harry stumbled into one of the Hackleburg potlucks several years ago on his way around the Rescue Mission circuit, he has developed an inner honing device that seems to send a signal whenever Hackleburg is about to have a potluck, even if he is a hundred miles away. He knows if he can make it back, Grandma Hester will say, "Son, you sit right down here and eat your full 'cause we have plenty."

So the people gathered and looked over the food and made the same remarks they make at every Hackleburg potluck: "Isn't God good?" "Aren't we blessed?" "There is enough here for the whole town." They talked about the diets they were going to start the next day, and how many times the preacher went through the line, and made comments about the excellent brownies sixth-grader Amy Steeth had brought and the seven-layer salad and Tillie Tilton's little loaves of bread and how Bill Schnect brought fish out of the Henderson pond and found the appleseed in Hester's pie. When the meal was over they shared the leftovers and filled their baskets. More than one remarked that they were carrying home more food than they had brought. And they laughed and had a good time, and then they went upstairs and sang carols and decorated the tree and heard Pastor Jameson talk about Jesus. When they went home they knew, whether they said it or not, that God loved them.

On Monday Pastor Jameson mentioned the potluck, Hester and all the pies to Clarabell Ingram at the nursing home. Clarabell is Hester's sister, about five years or so older. Some days Clarabell's mind slips, and she forgets things like what she had for lunch, or even if she had lunch. But other days Clarabell can remember things from long ago that she had not thought about for years. Monday was one of her remembering days.

"Hester always was a good cook . . . Ma taught us when we were young . . . Hester won the pie-baking contest at the Farmer's Institute when she was only eight." Then Clarabell thought, and laughed, "Preacher, did you ever hear about the time Hester took a pie to church?" Pastor Jameson looked at his watch; on the days Clarabell was in a remembering mode the pastoral call took an hour longer. He admitted he hadn't heard the story and settled into his chair.

Well, it was back in the Depression, 1933, I think. Let's see, I would have been fifteen. Maybe Hester was ten. Times were hard. It was a bad year, no rain in July and August, no crops, although the price wouldn't have been good anyway. In November the bank closed and people lost money. Our neighbor Mrs. Wilcox came over and talked to Ma and said she thought we would all die of starvation.

On Sunday before Thanksgiving, the preacher—it was that little roly-poly man, Rev. Whitko—he always had something to say—said to everybody: "Next Sunday night I thought it would be nice if we would have a potluck and thank God for all his goodness. So you all plan on it and bring a well-filled basket."

Pa wasn't happy with what Rev. Whitko had to say. He said on the way home, "It's easy for the preacher to talk that way; he doesn't grow any crops, he doesn't have a mortgage and he didn't lose any money in the bank." When Pa got home he just sat at the kitchen table with his head in his hands and said he was a failure. He never should have gone into farming. If God was good why did we have it so hard? He guessed there would be no Christmas this year. He wondered if we could even go back to church. Wondered if there was any use to carry on. Ma was crying.

Hester and I were scared, really scared. We had never seen Pa act that way. And so we went out in the barn and we talked.

Hester said, "We have to do something." "Well," I said, "sure, do something, but what?" Hester said, "We have to pray." So we prayed, and when that was done I said, "Now what?" Hester said, "We have to listen to what God says to us." "How do you do that?" I asked. "Well, we read our Bibles." So we got our Bibles and opened them and put our fingers down and figured that would be God's message. My verse was Ecclesiastes 10:9. Can you quote that preacher?

Clarabell laughed as the preacher shifted uncomfortably in his chair. She continued her narrative.

"Dead flies cause the ointment of the apothecary to send forth a stinking savour." I didn't like that one so I tried again and got Titus 1:12. You know what that is, preacher?

Pastor Jameson admitted he didn't.

"The Cretians are always liars, evil beasts, and slow bellies." I had no idea what a Cretian was, let alone a slow belly. So I gave up. But Hester, well, Hester opened up to Deuteronomy, chapter twenty-six. Do you know what that is, Preacher?

Pastor Jameson admitted he was a little vague on Deuteronomy.

It's about firstfruits. The first of all the fruits, you take that, and you put it in a basket, and you go to the place God is, and you give it to the priest, and the priest puts it down before the altar. Hester said, "That's what we have to do." I said, "For you maybe, not for me." Hester read a lot the next few days in Leviticus and Numbers about offerings to God, lambs without blemish and more about firstfruits. She couldn't figure out what firstfruits were. Then she was walking in the orchard and saw some leftover apples on the ground, and she said, "That's it, that's the firstfruits—apples. What did Adam and Eve have in the garden? Apples." She had to give God apples, but those apples were all full of scars and scabs and rotten spots. They certainly weren't without blemish. I told her, "Just cut out good pieces. Just the pieces have to be without blemish. Make a pie out of the good pieces."

So she did, on Saturday when Ma and Pa were in town. Used up all the sugar.

Clarabell laughed, thinking of her sister making that pie.

Ma and Pa came home. Pa says, "What's that?" "It's a pie for God." Pa said, "We aren't going to the potluck." Hester said, "It is for Sunday morning." Ma said, "You used up all the sugar?" Ma started to cry again. All the sugar was gone.

Well, we went to church. Hester had her pie in a basket. People looked at it, kind of strange. "What's in the basket, Hester?" Hester said, "Firstfruits." Nobody had any idea what firstfruits were so they just sort of shrugged their shoulders. When the offering plate was passed Hester put her basket right on top of the offering plate.

Clarabell had to laugh some more, remembering her little sister putting that basket on the offering plate.

They had to pass the plate all the way back. Everyone had to balance that basket on top of the plate and pass it down the pew. Ed Shiltess was ushering that day. He just shook his head and took the plate up and gave it to Rev. Whitko, that little roly-poly man. Rev. Whitko took the lid off the basket and reached in and brought out the pie. Some people thought that was kind of funny, but Rev. Whitko didn't laugh. He held that pie up.

"Once," he said, "Jesus was with a lot of people; they were there all day and they were hungry and there wasn't any food. I don't know why there wasn't any food. Maybe the crops were bad. Maybe the bank failed. Jesus said to the disciples, 'Go get some food.' They said, 'What do you mean? There is no food here. We don't have enough money.' Then Andrew said, 'There is a lad here, with five loaves and two fishes, but what are they among so many?'"

Then Rev. Whitko said, "We don't have five loaves and two fishes, but we have a pie, and we'll have something to eat tonight, if you come. Don't ever give up on God." And he took that pie, and laid it on the altar, and he said, "God, thank you, God, for the pie, which will feed us tonight." Nobody ever remembered anything else that happened that Sunday morning except that pie.

On the way home from church Pa didn't say anything but Ma was crying—she sure cried a lot that year—only this was a different kind of crying, she was hugging Hester and me and stroking Hester's hair. Finally, Pa said, "I think we ought to go to the potluck after all. Do we have anything to take?" Ma said, "What about turnips?" We didn't have much that year, but we had a garden full of turnips. So she cooked some and cut up some raw. I think the word got around about Hester and her pie because a lot of people showed up Sunday night that weren't there Sunday morning. I know our neighbor, Mrs. Wilcox, had some canned meat laid back and noodles. Mrs. Fraley said later, "We had a lot of sweet potatoes, nothing much else but sweet potatoes." Must have had a lot of people with apples because we had a lot of apple pies, and pumpkin pies, and raspberry pies. And potato salad. Mrs. Hooley baked five little loaves of bread, she said, just like the little boy with five loaves. And old John Fry went down to Henderson's pond and caught some fish, so we had fresh fish. We had loaves and fishes. There was more food there than anyone had ever seen.

Clarabell laughed. The more she thought about it, the more she laughed.

And everybody stood around and just looked at the food, and somebody said, "Isn't God good?" And I don't think I had heard anyone say for a long time that God is good. And they said, "Did you ever see so much food? Where did it all come from?" And somebody counted, and there were thirteen pies. A lot of pie was left over, but everybody wanted a piece of Hester's pie; they had to cut it in real little pieces. And the piece that Rev. Whitko got had an apple seed in it. He said, "Look, an apple seed." Hester was mortified, because it was supposed to be a pie without blemish. But

Rev. Whitko—Rev. Whitko always had something to say—said, "You know what this is? A Johnny Appleseed pie. Johnny Appleseed always left seeds around, because a seed represents hope. In every seed there is a tree, and if apple trees produce apples, we won't run out."

When we were all through eating, we gathered up the leftovers and shared them with each other and put them in the baskets everyone brought, and people said they were sure they took home more food than what they brought.

Then we went upstairs and sang Christmas songs and Rev. Whitko—he always had something to say—talked about firstfruits. The very best. And that's what happened at Christmas. God gave to us his firstfruits, Jesus, the very best he had.

Next week two of the older women, Mrs. Hatfield and Mrs. Gibson, came to Hester and told her they wanted her to serve on the Kitchen Committee, even though she was only ten years old. And she's been there ever since.

Now Clarabell really laughed, which was good because Clarabell hadn't had reason to laugh much since her husband Sam died two years ago. She laughed so hard the nurse came by to see if anything was wrong.

When she finished laughing she said, "Preacher, I so much enjoy our conversations." Of course Pastor Jameson had said hardly anything for the last hour. "You can pray now." And Pastor Jameson prayed. He thanked God for Hester, two Hesters, a ten-year-old little girl, and now a Grandma; for Clarabell; and for Rev. Whitko—a predecessor he had never known, a roly-poly man who always had something to say—and he thanked God for a little boy who offered his lunch to Jesus and a little girl who offered a pie, and for Hackleburg's being a thirteen-pie church.

CHAPTER FIVE

The Election of Connie Ashton

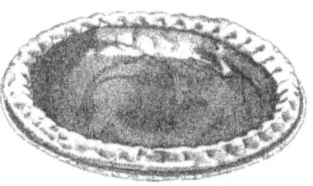

October 13, 1967

Most things are predictable at the Hackleburg Church. Charlie Purdin will sit every Sunday on the end of the fourth pew on the left side. The choir will sing "In the Garden" three times every year. Harry James will always be five minutes late to church. Delores Olmstead will complain at the Official Board meetings that the church is not dusted frequently enough. Billy John will always get converted all over again at the yearly revival. Hester Holloway will always bring an apple pie to the Hackleburg potluck. Hackleburg will get a new pastor every three years. On the predictability scale you can set your watches by Hackleburg traditions.

But the predictability scale went berserk when Connie Ashton was elected president of the WSCS (Woman's Society of Christian Service). Given the Hackleburg situation two weeks before the election, the odds of Connie's becoming president were about 500 to 1—not that Hackleburg people ever think in terms of odds. But all the women in the group will tell you today that a year ago they never would have dreamed that Connie Ashton would be president of the WSCS.

There were reasons for this, though none of the women would ever have admitted them. For starters Connie was not even a member of the church, let alone the women's group. Neither was Connie from any long-standing family in Hackleburg. In fact she and her husband Harry had been in Hackleburg only a short time. The Ashtons moved to Hackleburg when Mr. Ashton—that is, Harry—became part owner of the lumber yard in Pikeville. Hackleburg people are a bit suspicious of anyone who lives in Hackleburg who didn't grow up there or have business there, especially someone who works in Pikeville. The Ashtons had built a big new house on the bluff overlooking the Henderson Pond, a far nicer home than anyone in Hackleburg had thought appropriate. Furthermore, before coming to Hackleburg the Ashtons had been Episcopalian. People in Hackleburg didn't know much about Episcopalians, but someone said they were like Catholics, and Hackleburg people did know about Catholics. They got drunk on Saturday nights and then went to confession. They didn't eat meat on Fridays and they didn't sing songs like "I'll Fly Away."

Connie had come several times to the WSCS meetings, where she asked embarrassing questions like: "Now what is the purpose of this group?" No one had ever thought about that question before. And she asked, "Why do we always have a roll call with a response to some unusual question like, 'What is my favorite flower in the garden'?" The answer, which was, "Well, we've always done that," did not seem to satisfy Connie.

Furthermore, Connie was young. She was hardly forty and you never get a job like president of the WSCS when you are that young, though, as someone pointed out, when Marybelle took the job nearly fifty years ago she was that young. Finally, Connie talked with God. She talked with God all the time like God was right there in the room, like she was on a first-name basis with God, and the women of Hackleburg were a bit suspicious of that.

There needed to be an election in the WSCS because the person who had been president, Marybelle Hasselbaum, had died. She had died three weeks ago Tuesday from what appeared to be a heart attack. She was only eighty-two at the time. She had been to the store that very morning and had been working in her garden and that is where they had found her. Retracing her steps to the store and recounting how many people and what people had seen her there, how well her garden was weeded, how she looked several days before her death, how good it was to see her daughters at the funeral, and what a fine life she had led, having been president of the WSCS as well as the WCTU, had filled up the conversation time among the women for several weeks after the funeral, but now it was time to look ahead. Looking ahead meant "the women"—which is what they usually called the Woman's Society of Christian Service— needed a president. Marybelle had inherited the job from her mother, Bertha Littlejohn, who herself had been the founding mother of the Hackleburg Ladies' Aid Society and Foreign Missionary Society. When she died sometime before World War I Marybelle had taken her place.

But now Marybelle was gone. Some of the women were not exactly pleased that Marybelle hadn't told anybody she was going to die and she had not appointed anyone to take her place. Normally Marybelle planned ahead for emergencies like this. As it was, without any suggestions from Marybelle, there were no logical heirs. Marybelle had only had two daughters, but one lived in Pittsburgh and the other in California and thus they were not prospects to be the new president. Marybelle's sister Ethyl would have been a prospect but she had died last fall before Marybelle, so that wasn't going to work.

Everyone knew how important the WSCS was. There were wedding receptions to oversee, parsonage furnishings to consider, the church's best china to guard, kitchen policies to implement, noodles to be made for the annual chicken and noodle dinner, missions speakers to be invited, the altar to be decorated each Sunday, Christmas decorations to be put up every year, college students to be sent greetings and social times to plan. Marybelle had been responsible personally for each of these tasks. If one were to rank the importance of the leaders at the Hackleburg church, or in the Hackleburg community itself, the president of the Methodist women's group was right up there at the top along with the president of the Baptist Women's Missionary Society. After that you could argue about the trustees' job or the Sunday school superintendent or the chief of the volunteer fire department or the principal at the school. Somewhere down the list you could also consider the pastor.

So the WSCS group was in a quandary. Without a president the work of the church was in jeopardy, indeed the kingdom of God was in jeopardy. Two church members, Bill Swanke and Edna Hurley, were near death and would require a funeral dinner and at Edna's funeral dinner they would probably use the best china and at the moment there was no one with the authority to grant permission to use the china.

Pastor Wilson was anxious, too, that the position be filled and suggested that because of the importance of the position he would facilitate the election. It was his opinion that the group should ballot, since that was the way the Roman Catholics selected a pope, or Methodists selected bishops, and this job was of similar importance. They would have a meeting. Every woman would write down the name of the person she believed God would select for the job, and whoever had the most votes would be elected. This method would avoid embarrassment when a Nominating Committee would suggest one name and not others, or when people had to nominate from the floor and their friends might be upset if they were—or perhaps if they were not—nominated.

So on Tuesday the first of June, twenty-two members gathered to do their Christian duty, to ascertain God's will and select a new leader for their group. Their understanding of ascertaining God's will was to attempt to find someone willing to take the job.

"Nora, you would make a wonderful president." "No, I couldn't do that. You know how busy John is with milking cows and all." "Ruth, how about you? You speak so clearly." "Oh, I get so nervous in front of people." "Girls, don't you think that Delores would make a wonderful president?" "Oh yes, and Alberta would, too." "Sandra, you live close to the church. You could just run over to the church whenever anything needs to be done." While being president of the WSCS carried prestige, everyone realized that there would never be another Marybelle Hasselbaum, and whoever became president would be subject to a lot of criticism.

Finally, when everyone was totally confused, the first ballot was taken. There was a nervous several moments of talk about the weather and gardens and someone's new skirt while Pastor Wilson counted the votes.

Pastor Wilson came back and in a solemn voice announced the results: Minnie Rittenhouse, 1; Hester Holloway 1; Velma Hipsburg, 1; Nora Teegarden, 1; Sarah Arnold, 1; Alberta Havergale, 1; Goldie Samuels, 1; Marjorie Wooley, 1; Ruth Littlejohn, 1; Henrietta Hagley, 1; Delores Stuckey, 1. There were eleven abstentions. After a moment of silence someone near the back of the room said, "Heavens to Betsy!" and someone else on the left side said, "Glory Be!" And Minnie Rittenhouse said, "Mercy!" Ascertaining God's will was going to be more difficult than they imagined.

What had happened was that: (1) No one had voted for herself since in the Hackleburg way of doing things that would be considered bad manners; (2) In ascertaining God's will the women were not necessarily operating from the purest of motives. Ruth Littlejohn cast her vote for Henrietta Hagley not so much because she wanted Henrietta to be president but because she did not want Goldie Samuels elected. Hester Holloway voted for Sarah Arnold with the hopes that if Sarah became WSCS president she would give up the organist's job and the church could finally get someone who could play the organ. Delores Stuckey really wanted the job but did not want to vote for anyone who she considered was a front runner so she voted for Marjorie Wooley. Eleven people each received one vote. Eleven others were so rattled by indecision they turned in blank ballots.

At this point there was an awakening of what in Bible terms is called "the flesh," that is, human ambition. To be elected president of the WSCS would be a signal honor. A person could go to district meetings and be recognized. Her name would be mentioned in the church bulletin along with other important and powerful positions such as pastor, custodian and choir director.

It also occurred to each person who received votes that at least one other person had voted for her and if she had voted for herself she would have won the election. And so in a matter of moments reticence and humility and feelings of inadequacy and shyness were all overcome and at least eleven women began to wonder if maybe God had not called her to a bigger purpose in this fine hour and each one began to imagine what wonderful things she might accomplish if she were president. Velma Hipsburg never did like chicken and noodle dinners, and if she were president she could change to smelt for fund-raising dinners. Her husband, Bob, always went to Michigan in the spring for smelt and usually brought enough home to feed the whole church. Marjorie Wooley thought if she were president they could replace the dreadful blue curtains in the church parlor. Sarah Arnold believed if she were president she could get the women to buy new choir robes. Delores Stuckey wanted to have the monthly meetings changed from Tuesday to Wednesday so she could join a bridge club over in Pikeville. This time instead of a lot of talk about all the people who would make a good president there was silence as each one considered how she herself might make a good president.

The second ballot was taken. More nervousness and more talk about the weather and gardens while Pastor Wilson tallied and then read the results: Minnie Rittenhouse, 1; Hester Holloway, 1; Velma Hipsburg, 1; Nora Teegarden, 1; Sarah Arnold, 1; Alberta Havergale, 1; Goldie Samuels, 1; Marjorie Wooley, 1; Ruth Littlejohn, 1; Henrietta Hagley, 1; Delores Stuckey, 1. Eleven abstentions. From the back of the room came a barely audible "Heavens to Betsy!" and on the right side, "Glory Be!" Minnie Rittenhouse said, "Mercy!" Pastor Wilson made a comment about how every one must have turned in the exact same ballot. What he did not know was that apart from the abstentions, everyone who voted turned in a different ballot. Eleven women each voted for herself and there was another eleven-way tie.

At this point a cloud of despair entered the scene. The women were not of one mind. Each one was aware that no one had voted for her except she herself. The pastor's idea of balloting was not working. They could ballot all day and with complex feelings of jealousy and pride mingled with a sense of caring for one another and the group, they might never have a president and if they did, there would be a lot of hard feelings. No one really could fill Marybelle's shoes. They began to sense the disintegration of the group. What would become of them? The relationships in the group were so complex. They loved each other, yet the women were like sisters. They cared for one another and yet they antagonized one another. As long as Marybelle was president and making all the decisions peace reigned. Marybelle herself was the unifying force and now there was no unifying force, and it was possible they would soon be fractured in dozens of different ways.

At this point Connie Ashton made her speech: "We have spoken of God's will, but we have not prayed. Why don't we pray specifically that God would put in our minds the image of the person he wants for this job. We have so many wonderful women in this group. This is not our end. We should see this as our beginning. We put on the best meals in the county. We should use that for the glory of God. My husband works in Pikeville and let me tell you, the group at the church there cannot hold a candle to this group. We can double our pledge to missions. I don't know who God wants for president but let's wait on him. Let's pray and ask God to bring to our minds the right person."

From the back of the room came a barely audible, "Heavens to Betsy!" and from the right side came a "Glory be!" Minnie Rittenhouse said, "Mercy!" Pastor Wilson asked Connie if she would pray.

"Lord," Connie began, "you are going to have to pick the president of this group because we can't, so show us who it is. We have our eyes closed, and we want you to put that face right in front of us. And when the pick is made may the woman picked not refuse, but know it is God's will."

Connie suddenly felt very foolish. Why had she spoken? She had never been so bold. What right did she have to tell these people what to do? What if God didn't come through? She searched her own mind. She tried to think of all the women in the group. The only thing she thought she saw was what appeared to be a redheaded angel holding a mirror in front of her face. She didn't understand that at all, so she turned in a blank ballot.

Pastor Wilson gathered the ballots and once again there was nervous talk about the weather and the gardens. Then the pastor read the results. "There is one blank ballot. There are twenty-one votes for Connie Ashton." From the back of the room came a barely audible, "Heavens to Betsy!" From the right side came a barely audible, "Glory Be!" Minnie Rittenhouse said, "Mercy!" From the left side came "Hallelujah!" and then a spontaneous burst of hand-clapping. The women of Hackleburg had just seen the Red Sea parted, fire from heaven on Elijah's altar and water turned to wine.

Connie was undone. This was not the way this was supposed to turn out. She said, "O for goodness sakes." Then she said it again. And again.

That night Connie went home, faced her husband and had it out with God. "God, you tricked me." She and her husband took a crash course in Methodism and joined the church the next Sunday. And Connie joined the WSCS.

In the next two weeks Connie held ten teas in her home, her beautiful new home overlooking Henderson Pond. She invited three of the women of the WSCS to each tea. She made crumpets and served herbal tea and learned about Hackleburg and about the church and she found out about each woman. Then she talked with God.

Two weeks later was the regular meeting and Connie made her assignments. God had given every woman in that group a gift. Hester Holloway would oversee everything that happened in the kitchen. She would be personally responsible for the church potlucks. Alberta Havergale would work with her and would guard the china to make sure no unauthorized persons borrowed it. It was her responsibility to say who got to use it and who didn't. Goldie Samuels would coordinate all funeral dinners. Marjorie Wooley would do all wedding receptions. Henrietta Hagley would be responsible for the flowers on the altar each week. Delores Stuckey would do Christmas decorations. Nora Teegarden would do fund-raising dinners. Minnie Rittenhouse would work with the Sunday school superintendent and would do anything related to children. Velma Hipsburg would be correspondence secretary and would be in touch with all college students and service men and women. Connie herself would take the two hardest jobs, getting along with Otis Hankins and the trustees and with whoever the pastor happened to be. Ruth Littlejohn would keep the women informed about all missionary projects.

So everyone is happy. And the church will carry on.

CHAPTER SIX

The Little Short Pew by the Side Door

November 30, 1961

For twenty-three years Charlie and Marianne Johnson worshiped God in the Hackleburg Church while sitting in the little short pew by the side door. That is not particularly significant in the work of God's kingdom, except that it did offer Hackleburg believers a certain sense of security. Just as the picture of Jesus and the lambs had hung over the pulpit for as long as anyone could remember, so Charlie and Marianne sat in their pew.

Then late this past August, Charlie had a heart attack. Marianne stayed home to nurse Charlie back to health. And when Pastor Dilley began a fall sermon series on Exodus, the little short pew by the side door was empty.

On September 20, usher Mack Horine slipped out of the service to check the car windows against an impending rain storm. When he returned, he did not want to disturb

Moses in the bulrushes in Pastor Dilley's sermon, so he ju-
diciously sought refuge in the little pew by the side door.
Even before Moses escaped the bulrushes for Pharaoh's
palace, Mack decided the little short pew was an ideal usher's
pew. The spot by the side door was more convenient should
car windows need to be checked or some other emergency
arise. Furthermore, the little pew was more peaceful than
the fourth pew on the left side where he usually sat with his
wife Pam and three wiggly children.

On September 27, Julie Anderson, new kindergarten
teacher in town, brought herself and her two sons, Bobby
(age three) and Michael (age two) to church. She was pleased
to find the little short pew by the side door. Obviously, the
church had placed the pew there for the benefit of mothers
whose small sons might have to use the restroom during
Pastor Dilley's sermon. After three trips to the restroom,
two more for drinks, and one to deliver an old-fashioned
spanking (beautifully coordinated to enhance Pastor Dilley's
description of Egyptian taskmasters beating Hebrew slaves),
Julie saw the little short pew as the one glimmer of God's
grace in an otherwise unredeemed morning.

On October 4, J. J. Peterson, his leg in a cast after he
had failed spectacularly and ignominiously to rescue his son's
kite from the big maple tree, found the short pew by the side
door the ideal place for people with a handicapping condition. Julie Anderson was forced to sit in the ninth pew on
the left side. There, while Moses terrorized the Egyptians
with plagues, Bobby and Michael terrorized the old ladies
who usually sat in rows eight, nine and ten.

On October 11, Julie Anderson arrived for worship at
9:18 and claimed the little short pew. J. J. Peterson arrived
at 9:25, found the pew occupied, and became an instant
convert to social justice. While Moses railed against Pharaoh, he railed inwardly against those who discriminate
against the handicapped.

On October 18, J. J. Peterson claimed the little pew by the side door at 9:11. Julie Anderson, arriving at 9:19, sat again in the ninth pew on the left side where Bobby and Michael munched Cheerios out of a baby food jar while the Israelites in Pastor Dilley's sermon were eating unleavened bread. After a short time Bobby and Michael discovered a new pastime: smashing the Cheerios between pages of the hymnal.

On October 25, Julie Anderson arrived at 8:57 to claim the little short pew. J. J. Peterson arrived at 9:05 with a professionally printed sign saying, "Reserved for the Handicapped," and asked Julie to move. At 9:10 Mack Horine arrived with a professionally printed sign saying "Reserved for Ushers," and asked J. J. to move. At 9:17 Charlie and Marianne Johnson returned to church for the first time in two months. Charlie thought the usher sign was the most ridiculous thing he ever seen, removed it, and claimed the pew. Handicapped may outrank children, and ushers may outrank handicapped, but twenty-three years of tradition outranks everything.

Pastor Dilley at that point suddenly realized how Moses felt out in the desert with a thousand Egyptian chariots closing in. Being in his heart a peaceful man (and a schemer), the pastor asked Charlie and Marianne to come forward before the pastoral prayer and sit on the front pew so that proper thanks could be given to the Lord for Charlie's recovery (and so the little short pew by the side door would be vacated). There was no joy in the Lord's house that day.

On October 26, 27, 28, 29, 30 and 31, Pastor Dilley besought the Lord day and night, lest the church at Hackleburg be rent asunder. Surely the Lord had not brought the little band of believers this far into the desert only to be destroyed by Egyptian armies. With a burst of faith he claimed Exodus 14:13 as a promise: "Fear not, stand firm, and see the salvation of the Lord, which he will work for you today."

On November 1, when Pastor Dilley got up to preach, not a single person sat in the little short pew by the side door. Mack Horine's wife, Pam, had convinced Mack, usher or not, that his responsibility during Pastor Dilley's sermons was to sit with his family. Bobby and Michael Anderson had convinced their mother that the ninth pew on the left side was "their seat." The old ladies in rows eight, nine and ten had become grandmas who give out candy and there were "Cheerios in the songs." J. J. Peterson had his cast removed and returned to his old pew by the window.

Charlie Johnson told Marianne he had heard the sermon the Sunday before better than he had heard any sermon for the past eight years. He guessed it was because when they sat in the little pew by the side door he always had his bad ear toward the preacher. Charlie supposed he and Marianne ought to sit up near the front all the time.

The people who left Hackleburg church that day said it was one of the finest services they ever attended. The Lord had richly blessed. The pastor had preached on the parting of the Red Sea. Pastor Dilley added that the Lord still works miracles, and he was positive he had witnessed one in Hackleburg that very day.

CHAPTER SEVEN

The Baptism of Michael Anderson

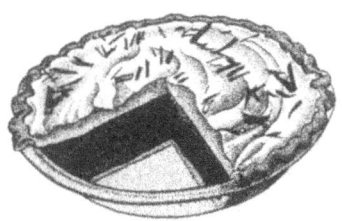

April 17, 1962

F or as long as anyone could remember, Aunt Minnie Rittenhouse has been the teacher for Jesus' Little Sunbeams at the Hackleburg church. Most of the people in Hackleburg who know about Moses in the bulrushes, the boy who gave his fishes to Jesus when people were hungry, and how Peter cut off a soldier's ear with a sword have heard it all from Aunt Minnie and her Big Blue Bible Story Book. Those who can sing—who know about climbing up sunshine mountain, how to be burning burning burning because there is oil in the lamp and how Jesus wants us for sunbeams—have sung with Aunt Minnie.

Because of Aunt Minnie, the children of Hackleburg and the children of those children can fold their hands and close their eyes and pray for pets and daddies and rain for the corn. Aunt Minnie knows what angels are like, how giraffes got on the ark and what kind of slingshot David used when he slew Goliath. (Goliath was always "slewed," not just struck or even killed.) Aunt Minnie also dispenses hugs and blessings and enough candy to increase tooth decay in Hackleburg by five percent.

Preachers and Sunday school superintendents come and go at Hackleburg church, but Aunt Minnie remains, a fixture in her rocking chair in the Jesus' Little Sunbeams classroom. Christian education professionals in high places develop new theories of teaching, write new curriculum materials and give lengthy discourses on changing times. But Aunt Minnie just reads the stories out of the Big Blue Bible Story Book. Jesus' Little Sunbeams grow into bigger sunbeams, then teenagers, then college students, and get married and have children who go to Sunday school to hear the same stories their parents heard.

When the young-married class had a debate over the number of lions in Daniel's den, someone was delegated to check with Aunt Minnie and the picture in the Big Blue Bible Story Book for the correct answer (four). When a group in the senior class sang "Climb, Climb Up Sunshine Mountain" for talent night at the high school, much of the whole school joined in and did the song with motions learned from Aunt Minnie.

None of this, however, had impressed itself upon Michael Anderson, age three. Michael did not like the Hackleburg nursery. For one thing it smelled like Grandma Peterson's basement and reminded him of cobwebs and dill pickles. For another thing Kathy Ricker wouldn't let him play with the toy trucks, and Sandy Sanderson always cried for her mommy. Michael didn't sing because he did not like the idea of burning burning burning (with or without oil), and he didn't want to be a sunbean (or any kind of bean for that matter).

Furthermore, Aunt Minnie hugged too hard, and she never called him Michael. She always called him "Mercy

Child," as in, "Mercy, child, you have crayon all over your face," or, "Mercy, child; you've had three pieces of candy already."

Of course, Aunt Minnie called most people either Mercy Child or Mercy something. When Pastor Jameson would come by the nursery, Aunt Minnie would say something like, "Mercy, Preacher, can't we get a little heat in here?" When Michael would find a piece of last week's candy on the floor, or some ants who had also found last week's candy, Aunt Minnie would say, "Mercy, those trustees." One day when a sparrow was flying around in the nursery, Aunt Minnie said mercy to the trustees and mercy to the sparrow and mercy to Sandy Sanderson who was screaming for her mommy.

Sometimes Aunt Minnie would even say mercy to God, like when she would read about how the stable smelled when Jesus was born and how mean men put nails in Jesus' hands. She would close the Big Blue Bible Story Book, give each of the children a hug, and say, "Mercy, Lord."

One Sunday Aunt Minnie greeted Michael at the nursery door with an exclamation: "Mercy, child, I've just discovered you've never been baptized!" Michael suspected something was wrong, like it was past bedtime and he hadn't had a bath yet or everyone was going for ice cream and he hadn't picked up his toys. When Pastor Jameson came by the nursery door, Aunt Minnie called out, "Mercy, Preacher." (Like Michael, Pastor Jameson suspected something was wrong whenever he heard, "Mercy, Preacher"— perhaps it was too cold in the nursery or his shirttail was out). Aunt Minnie exclaimed, "Do you know this child has never been baptized?"

From that point on, any concern the angels in heaven might have had about Michael Anderson's baptism were put to rest. Aunt Minnie had taken it upon herself to challenge principalities and powers on behalf of one of Jesus' Little Sunbeams.

That very day Aunt Minnie treated Jesus' Little Sunbeams to a theological dissertation on baptism. No matter that Pastor Jameson was himself a little fuzzy on the subject, or that a great part of the congregation discussed the subject mostly around whether baptism is best administered with or without the help of a rose. Though everyone else be ignorant, Jesus' Little Sunbeams would be enlightened.

Michael went home that day and told his mother about special children being brought to Jesus so he could touch them, about how mommies and daddies would have to explain to the angels whether they had taken their little boys and girls to Sunday school, how God washes sins away and that's what the water is for, and how when Sandy Sanderson was baptized she did something and it got Pastor Jameson's suit all messy. Michael also explained that, according to Aunt Minnie, baptism made everyone in the church brothers and sisters, even Sandy Sanderson. Michael didn't drink his milk that noon because he didn't want to have Sandy Sanderson for a sister.

The next Sunday Aunt Minnie read to Jesus' Little Sunbeams the story of John the Baptist baptizing Jesus. She showed the picture in the Big Blue Bible Story Book of John in his Daniel Boone outfit with the sleeves off, pouring water over Jesus, who had a pigeon sitting on his head. Jesus was all wet.

Michael didn't like the story very much. He didn't like being in a lake with his clothes on and he didn't like birds, especially birds that landed on your head. He figured that's why the sparrow had been in the nursery that day—somebody was getting baptized.

After not too many days Pastor Jameson came to Michael's house "to discuss the baptism." By the time Pastor Jameson had explained to Michael's mother that the water does not really save babies but just helps them get ready to be saved, Michael had driven his Hot Wheels around the sofa, under the dining-room table, into the hall closet and had parked it and himself behind the coats. If there were any pigeons flying around, they weren't going to find him.

The next day Michael's mother took him shopping "to get a new outfit for his baptism." Michael hoped it would be a Daniel Boone outfit without sleeves, but it wasn't. It was long blue pants and a white sweater. Michael thought it would not feel good at all if he had to wear it in a lake.

On Sunday, according to Grandpa Peterson, who had come to be present for the baptism, Michael was "difficult." He did not eat his Cheerios for breakfast, he spilled his milk, and he cried when he had to put on his long blue pants. He did not even take the stick of gum Grandma Peterson offered him. He insisted on wearing his Daniel Boone coonskin cap.

When they arrived at church Michael made sure his coonskin cap was on and then looked around to see if any pigeons were present. Instead he saw Aunt Minnie, who hugged him and said, "Mercy, child, your guardian angel is rejoicing today." Now Michael had an angel to look out for, not to mention birds, ponds and someone in a Daniel Boone outfit. He retreated by closing his eyes tightly and putting his head in his mother's lap.

When it was time for the baptism Michael had two eyes closed, one hand on his cap, one arm around his mommy's neck, and two tears trickling down his cheek. Pastor Jameson said something about a very special boy and about Jesus who loved children and being part of God's family. The cap slipped off, and Michael felt a wet something on his head. He put his hand up. It wasn't a bird, for which he was happy. It was a finger. He opened his eyes and looked right into Pastor Jameson's face.

Then he saw all the people. Aunt Minnie was there, smiling. Grandpa Peterson was smiling. Mrs. Nelson, who owned the big black dog down the street, was smiling. Kathy Ricker was there with her mommy and daddy, and they were all smiling. Mr. Nickleson, who worked in the grocery store, was smiling. Everybody in the whole church was looking at Michael and they were smiling. Almost everyone that is. Sandy Sanderson was standing on the pew with her thumb in her mouth just staring at him. Then she took her thumb out and very slowly waved. Michael let go of Pastor Jameson's finger and waved back.

Then Michael looked at Aunt Minnie and for some reason he thought of how bad the stable smelled when Jesus was born, and how much it must have hurt when the bad men put nails in Jesus' hands, and how he was a Jesus' Little Sunbean and maybe Sandy Sanderson wouldn't be such a terrible sister after all. He saw Aunt Minnie say to herself, "Mercy!" And Michael sighed, and smiled, and said out loud so all could hear, "Mercy!"

CHAPTER EIGHT

The Hackleburg Choir

December 26, 1960

The Hackleburg church does many things well. Music is not one of them. The exuberance level is not bad on some hymns, but the taste level is considerably down the scale, and the talent level is lower yet. The Hackleburg people do pretty well on hymns from the blue *Pentecostal Gospel Hymns #5* song book, such as "Throw Out the Lifeline," which they like even though they are a thousand miles from the nearest ocean. But the people have not yet mastered the intricacies of some of the hymns in the big blue "official" Methodist hymnal. This situation is not helped by the high expectations of newly appointed pastors who rotate in and out of the Hackleburg church about every third year and who have been trained that congregations should not sing the same old hymns all the time. They need to try new hymns.

And so there was the week last year when Pastor Ned Bergman introduced hymn #471:

We bear the strain of earthly care, / But bear it not alone;
*   Beside us walks our Brother Christ*
And makes our task His own.

Through din of market, whirl of wheels,
And thrust of driving trade,
*   We follow where the Master leads, / Serene and unafraid.*

About three measures into the first verse the congregation was feeling that they were bearing more "strain of earthly care" than they thought necessary. They were loyal Methodists and did their best to "follow the Master," or at least the organist, but by the beginning of the second verse the basses were wandering lost in the "din of the market" and "whirl of the wheels." They needed Brother Christ to help them bear this burden not alone. None of this passed unnoticed by the little kids on the second pew, who burst into giggles when Arthur Vanderweiss finally looked at his book to see if he had the right hymnal.

By verse four even Pastor Bergman was faltering. He was most grateful to Mrs. Arnold, the organist, and the alto section of the choir for carrying through to the last phrase of the hymn, "The Master's winsome call," such as it was.

That was last year. This year Pastor Jameson in March came home from a continuing education event where he learned that any congregation can sing good music if only given the chance. So Pastor Jameson gave Hackleburg the chance with an Easter hymn, #161:

"Welcome, happy morning;" / Age to age shall say:
"Hell today is vanquished, / Heaven is won today."
*   Lo! The dead is living . . .*

For Mrs. Arnold it is hard to welcome a happy morning, or any morning for that matter, in three sharps.

Mrs. Arnold usually wants three weeks to practice three sharps even if it is something like "Throw Out the Lifeline." But Mrs. Arnold is a loyal Methodist and has taken much abuse from pastors who through the years have chosen weird hymns and so she was determined not to complain—though she should have. She determined to do her best.

Her best was not enough. The happy morning was not well welcomed. First the back three pews on the left side gave up on the hymn, then the basses, then the right side of the sanctuary, and then Pastor Jameson himself, not having the gift of music, though he held on as long as he could. This left, basically, Mrs. Arnold on the organ and the altos in the choir, namely Velma Hipsburg and Aletha Grossy. For Velma and Aletha, whether or not there is talent or whether or not there is taste, there is always exuberance. This exuberance is for church music in general and for alto in particular. Alto for both of them is a mission, as if God called them to carry alto to the ends of the earth. Velma sings alto even when she teaches little kids in Sunday school, to the extent that numbers of Hackleburg children do not know the melody, only the alto part, to "Climb, Climb Up Sunshine Mountain."

Thus, when it appeared in the singing that hell was not being vanquished nor heaven being won, Velma, with Aletha's help, and cheering from the angels in heaven, carried on, single-handedly, dragging Mrs. Arnold and the organ with them, to the grand finale, "Lo, the dead is living." It was a marvelous performance, eliciting cheers from the angels and sighs of relief from the congregation. They had made it through another new hymn.

All of this was unknown to Lisa Bailey, recent graduate of the Music Department of the state university and newly arrived in Hackleburg to take her first real job as the music teacher for the Hackleburg elementary school. Before she even had a chance to unpack in her new little yellow house over on Elm Street, she was asked by Pastor Jameson to direct the choir. Lisa, with high ideals of service and community involvement and hoping for acceptance in her new community, was honored. Maybe people in Hackleburg had heard that she had been soloist in the University Glee Club and had done research on the *Passions* of Johann Sebastian Bach. Like many music majors Lisa was an aspiring director, seeing herself in her imagination before a great robed choir, singing the *Passion According to St. Matthew,* by Bach, in the original German.

The truth is that the only word that had preceded Lisa to town was a word passed from Joe Barnhart, school board member, to his wife, Alberta, and then to Josephine, Pastor Jameson's wife, and finally to Pastor Jameson, that the new elementary school music teacher was moving into the Bud Francis house on Elm Street. Pastor Jameson was overjoyed, convinced that the Lord had heard his prayers and was immediately inspired to make a new-resident pastoral contact.

You see, the Hackleburg choir had fallen into such dire straits that they had been reduced to the ultimate indignity of having to have the pastor himself, who did not have the gift of music, to be the director. He was an interim director but his interim responsibilities had lasted for nearly a full year, or ever since he arrived in town. This is why he was camped out on the doorstep at the little yellow house when Lisa's U-Haul pulled up. He even helped unload a few pieces, not normally a task he was inclined to do, before he popped the important question about whether Lisa might be willing to consider the position of director of the Hackleburg church choir.

Lisa was impressed. This was a friendly community. The Methodist pastor had visited her before she was even unloaded and had wanted her to direct the choir. What Lisa, freshly scrubbed college graduate, enthusiastic about her place in the adult world and all of twenty-three years old, did not know was that it was no special honor to be asked to direct the church choir. Far lesser persons had been begged to take the job and had turned it down.

But Lisa's exuberance level was high and was not lowered even after a talk with Mrs. Arnold, the organist, who though she had been organist for twenty-three years, still disdained sharps and flats, let alone music written in German, and mentioned songs she liked that Lisa, with all of her college training, did not recognize, such as "Do You Slumber in Your Tent, Christian Soldier?" and "Let the Lower Lights Be Burning."

Nor was Lisa's exuberance lessened by what she found in what they called the "music room," which at Hackleburg also served as primary Sunday school classroom and storage closet for an assortment of Bible costumes that are called into service whenever the church does a skit or a play featuring Bible characters. Lisa did not find the *Passions* of Bach, in German or in English, nor was there much else that she recognized, not being familiar with Stamps-Baxter and anthem books like *Southern Gospel on the Old Camp Ground,* but there were some anthems, from the 1920s she guessed, including a Christmas anthem about donkeys on the straw in the stable stall, that would be enough to get started.

But Lisa's exuberance level was destined to drop, and so it did—going into a free fall actually—about halfway through Hackleburg's first September rehearsal. By then Lisa had found out about the altos, in whose presence no PA system was ever needed, and about the sopranos, the basses, the tenors and the organist. And this after they had sung through music they already supposedly knew, like "Church in the Wildwood," which had been sung four times as an anthem the previous year.

Nora Teegarden, soprano, was sharp on high notes. Her sidekick, Alma Goodson, was flat on low notes and some notes in the middle as well. What Lisa thought was a sticking

B-flat key on the organ was really Harry Elworthy, who seemed to sing some part not written in the music but hovering mainly around B-flat, even when the music was written in C. Arthur Vanderweiss, the main bass, could sing on key, but like Beethoven of old, was growing deaf in his old age and was not always able to hear the starting pitch, particularly when he sat close to Harry Elworthy.

Worse, the choir did not seem particularly troubled by how terrible they were. Here they were facing a major crisis, the crisis being that they were supposed to sing something the week after next Sunday, and they were having a marvelous time, rehearsal serving for them not only a musical but also a social function. They visited when they should have been singing, gabbing about Eleanor Nelson's new baby, the corn's need of rain and whoever had bought the old Olmstead home on Walnut street, all to the chagrin of Lisa, who thought choir practice was supposed to have something to do with music.

By the end of rehearsal the second week Lisa was in ontological despair. That's the theological term for depression mixed with panic. Why was she standing before this strange group of people in this strange community singing these strange songs? The choir was scheduled to sing Sunday, and there was nothing to sing. They had never told her in college about choirs that were able to go sharp and flat at the same time, about amplified altos, monotone tenors, deaf basses and organists who despised sharps. What if her parents came to Hackleburg to visit and heard her choir? They would think all the money they had spent on her college education had been wasted. For all her pretending, the choir was beginning to catch on that Lisa knew nothing about church choirs, especially small-town church choirs who didn't know how to sing and didn't even know it. She had never heard of songs like "I'll Fly Away" and "Brighten the Corner Where You Are." Soon they would discover she had really not been in church very often in her life, and she didn't really know what this God business was all about.

Then Lisa did the last thing in the world she wanted to do, what she struggled against, something that would not impress people that she was a competent professional: She wept. She wept in uncontrollable sobs. Right in the middle of choir rehearsal. It was the lowest moment in her still young life.

Arthur Vanderweiss rescued her. Arthur, though getting deaf, was still wise. He suggested Lisa might sing a solo Sunday instead of the choir. Perhaps she could sing one of his favorites, one his mother liked, "His Eye Is on the Sparrow." Well, Lisa stayed after choir to learn the song and Arthur stayed in order to help her get the feel of it, and as might have been expected, almost all the choir hung around also because, if you want to know the truth, people in Hackleburg are reluctant to be the first ones to leave a meeting because they might miss something important or somebody might talk about them.

First Arthur sang the song and then Lisa sang it.

Why should I feel discouraged?
Why should the shadows fall? . . .
When Jesus is my portion, / My constant friend is He.
His eye is on the sparrow, / and I know He watches me.

Then Arthur sang it a second time and Lisa a second time. Lisa imagined the sparrow and God watching it, and she sang a third time with the voice God gave her that also was the voice that was the reason why she was soloist with the college chorale. She sang with a voice that dredged up from Arthur a lot of things he had forgotten, things about his mother and the church and God. It was Arthur's turn to shed tears, and when Arthur wept Nora Teegarden began to weep and then Velma Hipsburg. Lisa was touched.

People had clapped before when she sang, but no one had ever wept before.

Then from somewhere someone produced some old worn red song books and Mrs. Arnold played and they began to sing through the book: "Blessed quietness, holy quietness,/What assurance in my soul!" and "Ring the bells of heaven—there is joy today,/For the wand'rer now is reconciled."

Well, that was a long rehearsal if you want to call it a rehearsal. They just sang and sang. And the angels in heaven were kind of cranking up those bells in heaven. By the time they reached,

I am coming to the cross. / I am poor, and weak, and blind; . . .

Lisa began to feel she was not among strange people in a strange place singing strange songs to a strange God, for the words became her words:

I am counting all but dross; I shall full salvation find.

Before they went home that night, Arthur gave a closing prayer. He thanked God for Lisa, for bringing her to Hackleburg, and prayed that when she sang Sunday she would be a blessing, and someone would be touched.

When Sunday morning came Arthur introduced Lisa and expressed how blessed they were that Lisa had come to be with them, and that she was going to sing a song he requested because it was his mother's song. Lisa didn't perform as she had with the university chorale. She just sang what she had felt a few nights before, and the choir got touched all over again. The congregation was touched as well.

That noon, after Sunday dinner, a most unexpected thing happened. Janet Jameson, fourteen-year-old daughter of Pastor and Josephine Jameson, shocked her parents. Unlike her father, she had the gift of music, but had never exercised it, especially in church and especially around her parents. It was a thirty-volt shock. She declared that she had really liked Lisa Bailey's song, and she liked Lisa and wondered if she could be a part of the Hackleburg choir. The pastor was so excited he made eight pastoral calls on Sunday afternoon.

Well the choir sang, "His Eye Is on the Sparrow" three times in the next three months. Lisa did a solo one more time, Arthur sang a solo once and Janet Jameson sang once. The choir didn't try to perform; they just sang, and were fascinated by the things Lisa tried. She encouraged Aletha to consider herself a missionary to the tenors, and stood her beside Harry Elworthy, where the sheer power of her voice sort of transformed, or at least drowned out, Harry's B-flat. Velma carried alto all by herself. She could have carried alto by herself in the Marine Band. Arthur stood by the organ amplifier so he could start on the right pitch. Lisa put Janet Jameson between Nora and Alma, beside two experienced singers, as she explained, but actually so that Janet's clear and true voice would help keep Nora and Alma on pitch.

It was nothing too great, but respectable, so that by the time Christmas came, the choir, for the first time in many years, did a Christmas program. They fished out the old robes and got them cleaned. With a great leap of faith, they decided to do something rather daring. They learned "Silent Night" in German, and Lisa had her dream fulfilled, standing before a great robed choir singing in German. Her parents visited and were so proud, thinking the money they had invested in the college education was all worthwhile. And the angels in heaven, who had the gift of music, those who had been assigned to the Hackleburg church and who had suffered through the years, rang once again the bells of heaven.

CHAPTER NINE

The Travels of the Jesus' Little Sunbeams' Sandbox

August 6, 1984

T hey found the sandbox—the Jesus' Little Sunbeams' sandbox. It was in the old coal bin in one of those corners where no one bothers to look except once every six months or so when searching for the Bible costumes for the Christmas play or for the signs advertising the smelt supper. Generally things don't get thrown away at the Hackleburg church, but that does not mean anyone knows where they are. The sandbox was under a ten-year accumulation of broken tables and chairs that the trustees were going to get fixed one of these days. The sandbox had some coal dust grime and some cob webs and smelled like dead mice but was none the worse for wear. That sandbox had been built to last for two centuries, or for the coming of the Lord, whichever came first, and could easily endure ten years of neglect. So there it was, made of solid two-by-fours, reinforced, with a deep tin-lined basin, big enough so that four children—or more in cases of emergencies—can stand around it and make roads, drive cars, march soldiers and fill teacups with sand.

The sandbox was found just in time. One family, the Henrys, was about to leave the church if that sandbox had not been found. They were sure that the last time it was supposedly stored Tim Whitaker, the custodian and the sworn enemy of sandboxes, had secretly, by night, thrown it in the dumpster to end its life forever, and the Henrys were convinced that any church with such a callous view of God's holy vessels had betrayed the faith and was not worthy of their presence.

So everyone is happy again, relatively speaking. There is general agreement that the sandbox needed to come out of retirement and be returned to its rightful place in the northwest corner of the Jesus' Little Sunbeams' Sunday school room. And it should not only be returned but given respect: maybe painted and replenished with an adequate supply of sand from the Henderson Pond shore, so that it could be introduced to a new generation of Jesus' Little Sunbeams who had never had the privilege of pouring sand from one little teacup to another and telling the Christmas story with little figurines of wise men marching through the desert sand and shepherds running in from the desert hills and, as more than one person observed, marking the sanctuary carpet, the carpet in the Come-Join-Us adult Sunday school class and the linoleum in the kitchen with sand tracks where Jesus' Little Sunbeams had also tracked through the desert. If parents lost their little kids in the church they could just follow the sand tracks.

This outpouring of interest in the ministry of the sandbox is the direct result of a special gift from the Bibleland Modern Artifacts Manufacturing Company out of Pittsburgh, compliments of Patricia Schlosky. The gift, which arrived last Thursday in five big boxes, consisted of a complete line of products from the Bibleland Modern Artifacts Manufacturing Company, including sets of figurines of Bible characters, both Old and New Testament, along with some other Bibleland props such as Noah's Ark, a fiery furnace for Daniel's friends and Jacob's well. The Modern Artifacts Manufacturing Company is the major supplier to Christian book stores, as well as the street peddlers in Jerusalem, who sell figurines to tourists from Pittsburgh who travel halfway around the world to buy artifacts made in their own city. Bibleland Artifacts Manufacturing (BAM for short) products are also suitable as knickknacks for Christian families to put on shelves in their homes, as gifts from Sunday school teachers to third graders at Christmas or for church sandboxes.

Patricia Schlosky, donor of the set of Bibleland items, is a former Hackleburg girl who made it big in Christian ministry, in a humble sort of way, as one of the Bibleland Artifacts artists. Patricia actually creates the figurines, like little sheep and camels for Christmas manger scenes. Last summer Patricia was featured on the cover of *Christian Supply and Equipment* magazine. In the article about her, which has now hung for a number of months on the bulletin board by the men's restroom, she talks about the Hackleburg church and gives credit for her ministry in creative Christian knickknacks to the sandbox in the Jesus' Little Sunbeams' Sunday school room, where, according to the article, she spent hours as a child creating in sand the very figurines now shown in the Bibleland Modern Artifacts catalog.

A story like that touches a lot of hearts and so, particularly after the special gift arrived, the Hackleburg people, whatever their past feelings, revived their interest in the ministry of the sandbox and lamented their lack of vision for depriving a whole generation of its ministry, in fact two generations, of Jesus' Little Sunbeams. That's what started the hunt for the sandbox.

There are a lot of conflicting stories in Hackleburg, none of which is really true, about how the church came to have a sandbox, who made it and where it came from. It is not true, for example, that the sandbox was originally a horse trough at Sam Hilding's grandfather's farm, nor that it was once a kitty-litter box from the animal shelter over in Pikeville. People are aware that it is old because someone discovered that it has been mentioned in the church board minutes on numerous occasions as far back as they have board minutes, which is 1911.

The truth is that the sandbox was originally intended to be the tabernacle in the wilderness. Back in 1910 William Sprague was gloriously converted during the annual revival meeting. P. P. Baumgardner was the evangelist. P. P. challenged the people to tithe their income, read their Bibles and offer their talents in service to God. William and his wife Rachael weren't sure about the tithing part but they would try the Bible and the talents part.

So William started in the Bible in Genesis 1. He struggled through Noah's flood, Jacob's ladder and Moses floating down the Nile River in a basket, being mostly un-inspired. Then he got to Exodus 25. When he read about the tabernacle in the wilderness William got blessed. As far as anyone knows he has been the only person in Hackleburg's history, or in most church's histories, to get blessed by Exodus 25.

There he read about the offerings of gold and silver, scarlet goats' hair and rams' skin dyed red, badgers' skins, shittim wood and onyx stones, all to be made into a house of God, and with cunning work bowls made like almonds, knops, flowers, tongs, snuff dishes, fine linen, cherubim, boards for the tabernacle of shittim wood standing up, basins, fleshhooks and firepans. In his mind William saw it all laid out before him for the glory of God. And William said, "We've got to have one of those things right here in Hackleburg, maybe right out there in the backyard of the church." He shared his vision with Rev. Hendrickson who, in his discreet way, was appalled. He didn't want to question a vision from God. On the other hand he suspected that if anything like that showed up in the church backyard their church would be the laughing stock of the entire Hackleburg community, to say nothing of the Methodist conference.

The church board, when they heard the idea, was less kind, basically communicating the sense that this was the most ridiculous thing they had ever heard. For one thing the space behind the church was only one-fourth of what was needed for an authentic tabernacle, and furthermore where would William find the badgers' skins, let alone shittim wood and onyx.

So William began to scale down. A life-sized tabernacle became a reduced-sized tabernacle that became an inside tabletop tabernacle that, scaled down even more, became just the desert where the tabernacle stood. As in sand in a box where people could be creative in their own way and make their own fleshhooks and firepans and tongs and snuff dishes. So William used his God-given talent to construct what he called a desert place where the tabernacle could stand, but which everyone else called a sandbox. No matter, sandbox or whatever, it would be worthy of God. He made it out of solid walnut, polished it, reinforced its legs with cross pieces, lined the inside with tin and filled it with sand from the Henderson pond beach. He brought that sandbox into the church and put it in the old ladies' FaHoCha classroom (FaHoCha stands for Faith, Hope and Charity), where it lasted all of one week.

The ladies of the FaHoCha Sunday school class really didn't take to the idea of learning about the tabernacle in the wilderness from the big box filled with sand, especially since the box was put there without their approval. But the tabernacle box was an immediate hit with the little kids. Kids swarmed that sandbox the first Sunday and refused to go to Sunday school class. They were fascinated by William's showing them the little pieces of fleshhooks and firepans, and soon they were rearranging the tabernacle, improving a bit on Exodus 25, so that sand got spilled and was grinding into the carpet the FaHoCha class tried so hard to keep clean.

That's when the sandbox got moved down to the church basement, where the Jesus' Little Sunbeams' class met. Within the second week the sunbeams had gone beyond the tabernacle in the wilderness and were pushing little horses and wagons around, filling up little teacups and saucers and making the sandbox into the sensation of Hackleburg. By the third week kids were coming to Sunday school who hadn't been there for ages, and little Baptists were asking their parents if they couldn't become little Methodists. The whole thing led to a kind of revival in the Hackleburg Sunday school.

Which was actually rather short-lived. When revival hits, the Devil works overtime, in this case through the first and second graders, the third and fourth graders, brothers and sisters of Jesus' Little Sunbeams, graduates of the Jesus' Little Sunbeams' nursery class, who felt deprived that they weren't learning about the tabernacle in the wilderness and getting to push little buggies around in the sand. So they "horned in," in the words of one parent, and took over whenever they had a chance. Whatever lessons about sharing and being kind and loving one another were being taught in Sunday school were being offset by evidences of original sin, so that life around the sandbox sounded a lot like life at home: "Hey, I was here first." "It's my turn now." "Moth . . . er." "Teach . . . er." Parents were finding more and more of Henderson's pond sand in their children's hair and clothes when their kids came home from Sunday school.

That first year they went through three teachers in the Jesus' Little Sunbeams' Sunday school class. Bertha Hardy couldn't take the pressure of refereeing between kids. It was hard enough to corral her own grandkids without having to handle all the Methodist kids in Sunday school, let alone the Baptist kids. Her replacement, Mary Shepherd, lasted one week after Jesus' Little Sunbeams had discovered that sand could not only be poured into tea cups but into offering plates and the pencil holders and into the teacher's purse. Her replacement, Henrietta Hardcastle, solved the problem by simply removing the sand. The box was there but the sand was gone.

No problem. Hackleburg kids are creative. Little Johnny Hornsby declared if they couldn't have a desert they could have an ocean so with the help of his older brother Billy, a fourth grader, they brought water from the pump and created the Sea of Galilee, which floated little boats and sticks and pencils. Sometimes they had storms on the sea and a lot of the water from the Sea of Galilee got on the kids and on their clothes and on the floor and on the teacher and on the furniture.

That was when they found the Jesus' Little Sunbeams' sandbox out by the side lot, where after a good April rain that year, the sandbox turned into a kind of horse trough which the horses used to good advantage.

Now that might have been the end of the sandbox forever, except that William Sprague's feelings had to be considered, as well as Johnny Hornsby's mother, who for the first time in about four years hadn't had to yell and scream to get Johnny to come to Sunday school. The sandbox, or, that is, the desert box for the tabernacle, had been a great idea, that is, if the church had more committed and creative teachers. William was all willing to show them about the shittim wood and the fleshhooks if they would have him.

The May 12, 1912, minutes of the church board recorded these words: "It seemed best not to throw the sandbox away but to put it aside for a while until the Sunday school teachers could decide how best to make use of it." The vote was ten to four with two abstentions. So the sandbox was moved to the little shed out behind the outhouses.

That is where it was rediscovered about twenty-one months later by the twins Helen and Marianne Dorris, who lived across the street from the church, and Otis Hankins, and the gang on Walnut Street, who used the church backyard as a kind of town playground. Helen, Marianne and Otis, all age five but mature beyond their years, knew a blessing from God when they saw one, and when they were snooping around in the shed in the church backyard one day, they found one. A blessing. Whatever that big box was, they knew it was made for kids and they were kids, and before the day was over, they had their mothers and the preacher and even Hilda Jennings of the Old Ladies FaHoCha class—despite all that the FaHoCha class had endured—convinced that for the good of the church, the advancement of the kingdom, the angels in heaven and the glory of God, the sandbox belonged not in the shed behind the outhouses but in the Jesus' Little Sunbeams' Sunday school class.

Enthusiasm can overcome reluctance and even common sense, and the new generation of Jesus' Little Sunbeams were on an enthusiastic crusade. Within that very week the sandbox was back in the Jesus' Little Sunbeams' class in the corner of the basement, with sand from Henderson's Pond, and William Sprague was back explaining all about offerings of gold and silver and the tabernacle built of shittim wood.

Those were glory years for the church. The Sunday school began to grow, and the sandbox was part of the reason. Edna Hayfield, the teacher of Jesus' Little Sunbeams, made use of it for teaching. Her husband Harry carved little Bible figures, and Edna used those figures to tell the stories of Paul being let down out of the city on a rope, Joshua marching around Jericho and Jesus healing the blind man. One week when Edna didn't show up for class kids did the Joshua story themselves, with some enhancement. The walls of Jericho became real walls with blocks and books and the wastebasket all piled up. The walls were built so they could fall down and everything inside could get destructed. The walls fell again and again and each time more and more stuff got destructed—the pencils, the little buggies, the rebellious people, the Baptists, the teacups, the wise men and the song books. Actually the whole Jesus' Little Sunbeams' classroom was destructed, and that's when the sandbox was placed in the corner behind the furnace.

Sometime after that it showed up again only to be put away again. According to the church minutes of November 1919, there was a motion by Bill Olmstead and seconded by Martha Young that the sandbox be placed in the upstairs closet until further notice. The story is that Andrew and Matthew Cassady, the rambunctious and uncontrollable preachers' kids, had carried over some disagreement at home into the church and into the Jesus Little Sunbeams' class room where it involved all the Jesus' Little Sunbeams who decided to settle the World War in the classroom with sandbox mud balls as the weapons of choice. Henderson's pond beach sand makes marvelous mud balls when wet and it appeared there was more mud in the church than outside at the pond.

On January 10, 1927, there was mention in the church minutes without explanation that the church was thankful to Harry Golding for repainting the sandbox and returning it to the Jesus' Little Sunbeams' Sunday school room. On

July 8, 1927, there was mention that the janitor, Johnny Baker, had quit and the church needed a new janitor. Without explanation it was also mentioned that the sandbox was being stored in Nelson Johnson's barn east of town.

In the April 13, 1936, minutes of the board, Ann Golding reported on a wonderful Sunday school workshop she had attended in Pikeville where they spoke about creative ways of teaching Bible stories: pictures and flannelgraph and puppets and sandboxes. Then the minutes recorded: "There was a long discussion about the sandbox with no action taken." The May minutes of that year also recorded a discussion with no action taken, as did the June minutes, the July minutes and the August minutes. In the September 1936 minutes it was recorded that someone had moved the sandbox into the Jesus' Little Sunbeams' classroom without authorization from the board. However, attendance in the Jesus' Little Sunbeams' class had increased from three to nine, and so it was moved that the sandbox stay. The vote was nine to six with three abstentions.

In the August 1947 minutes it was recorded that the sandbox had been placed in the church barn. It was also mentioned that the trustees were trying to find someone who could tell them whether a piano's sound board that is buried in sand poured in from the top of the piano was ruined or could be restored.

In December 1950 the church was faced with an out-of-control Jesus' Little Sunbeams' Sunday school class. Its ringleaders were Billy McPherson and Eddie Jarrett, full of more exuberant energy than the teachers in Hackleburg had ever experienced. Maybe the sandbox would help direct the energy. Aunt Minnie Rittenhouse was the Jesus' Little Sunbeams' teacher and volunteered to be responsible for the sandbox if it could be returned to its God-appointed place. Those were glory years for the sandbox. A whole Hackleburg culture built up around the sandbox. The boys and girls could take turns. The girls had a doll house, in fact, two doll houses and furniture and drove little cars between the houses. The boys had a barn with little figures of cows and horses and pigs. During Sunday school time the barn could double as Noah's Ark and the doll houses as the temple in Jerusalem where Jesus went when he was twelve years old before he got separated from his parents.

In March 1953 the sandbox was stored in the closet with the mops and mop buckets. In July 1960 the sandbox was cleaned up, painted and returned to Aunt Minnie Rittenhouse and Jesus' Little Sunbeams, to the joy of the junior high class, the same group that was responsible for causing it to be removed seven years previous, who now spoke of how great Sunday school was in the "olden days" when Aunt Minnie Rittenhouse used little figures to act out Bible stories like the Good Samaritan and Samson slaying the Philistines with a jaw bone (remembering with nostalgia that Aunt Minnie had a real jaw bone that had probably belonged to a raccoon).

In 1965 the church minutes read that the sandbox would be stored behind the old furnace until further notice. In 1974 the sandbox was returned to the Jesus' Little Sunbeams after a group of high school students gave testimony at church camp about coming to believe in Jesus as children playing in the nursery around the sandbox with Aunt Minnie Rittenhouse.

Sometime between 1974 and 1988 the sandbox disappeared again. They didn't record it in the church minutes. It might have been forgotten if it not been for Patricia Schlosky and last week's gift from the Bibleland Modern Artifacts Manufacturing Company. Whatever its problems in the past, the sandbox is back. People in Hackleburg believe in forgiveness and all of its past sins are forgiven. There was a celebration of sorts to recognize its return, sort of like when the Ark of the Covenant was brought to

Jerusalem. People rubbed their hands over it and treated it like a long-lost friend.

Henry Holman was the person who restored it. He said he stripped off eight layers of paint and found solid walnut underneath. He also found a name, W. Sprague, 1911, and an inscription, "The Tabernacle in the Wilderness." William was Mary Willis' grandfather, and Mary was ecstatic. She now knew what the little box of hand crafted pieces was that her grandfather had been so proud of. She looked up Exodus 25: fleshhooks and shittim wood and badger skins. One of the boxes from the Bibleland Modern Artifacts Company had a little box labeled "furniture for the tabernacle in the wilderness," with an altar and candlesticks and pillars of shittim wood and fleshhooks.

So it will be there, fully equipped when Patricia Schlosky makes a visit to Hackleburg to visit her cousin. She'll want to see that sandbox. Everyone is happy—at least until further notice.

CHAPTER TEN

Otis and the Barn

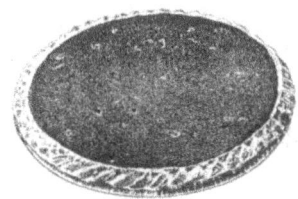

October 3, 1976

Nobody in Hackleburg can remember back before there was a barn that stood at the back of the lot beside the church. The barn was just always there, part of the Hackleburg landscape, like the crack in the sidewalk in front of Ed Baker's house or the big sycamore tree next to the town sign on the township road. In the early summer people commented about the beautiful hollyhocks that surrounded the barn, but other than that, the barn drew little attention.

Sometime in its distant past the barn sheltered horses and cows and chickens and who knows what else and was a place of activity, or at least people assumed that was so. In its more recent past, say, in the last seventy-five years, it mostly just accumulated "things"—things from the town park, for which it served as a sort of maintenance barn, things from the church, things from its previous owner and things from Otis Hankins, its caretaker.

Lush Larkin was the town scoundrel who years ago got saved and got rich, though not necessarily in that order, and willed to the church his earthly possessions including the field that became the town park, the official name of which, as is stated on the monument at the park's entrance, is The Lush Larkin Hackleburg Memorial Methodist Episcopal Glory to God Bible Wonderland Hollyhock Municipal Park. The church also, whether it wanted it or not, inherited a stuffed dog, Susanna, the barn, a house and Otis Hankins.

Otis, for reasons not quite clear in the minds of most people, administered a trust fund set aside for upkeep of the park and ended up living in the house. He also, over the course of time, became known not only as head trustee at the church but as Mr. Hackleburg himself. The town needed things to be done and Otis was available. Otis eventually became not only caretaker of the park, Park Superintendent, and Park Maintenance man but also Head of the Street Department, Superintendent of the Fire Station, the Town Marshal and Head of the Sanitation Department. He kept accounts of his various responsibilities in different drawers in his living room desk where things sometimes got mixed up so that people were usually uncertain as to what was in the church trustee fund, what was in the park fund, what was in the town street or fire department fund, and what was in Otis' personal fund.

Otis was also the keeper of the barn and the items therein, such as the current lawn mower for the park and the church, the lawn mower before that, which didn't work and the lawn mower before that, which also didn't work.

In addition to the lawn mowers the barn stored old tires, broken tables from the church that the trustees were always intending to fix, discarded church parlor furniture from years gone by, accumulated items dating back to Lush Larkin and lots of newspapers.

The newspapers dated back to World War II or earlier, when recycling newspapers was part of the strategy to win World War II. The youth group had collected lots of papers and Pastor Ed Ferguson, a born gambler, convinced the youth they should outwit the paper recycling market by stockpiling the papers in the barn until the price went up. Well, Pastor Ferguson, in true Methodist style, was reappointed, the price never went up, the youth group went on to bigger things and the papers remained in the barn. Lots of papers. One reason most church members complained little about the barn was because they knew if they said too much about cleaning up the place they would be responsible for the papers, as well as the worn-out lawn mowers and other assorted items they had no desire to know about.

It is not that no one ever went in the barn; it is just that when persons entered the barn they faced a maze of paths and tunnels between the papers and the old tires and the old parlor furniture, and they came out saying, "God deliver us." And they wondered about Otis, who had little concern about the disarray of the barn, but who, as head trustee, seemed obsessed about order and cleanliness and rules when it came to the church.

One by-product of Otis' desire for order and cleanliness was the signs—hand-printed instructions and reminders tacked here and there about how life was to operate inside the church building. While some congregations put out a welcome mat or some other reminder that theirs was a friendly church, Hackleburg visitors were greeted at the front door with a hand-printed sign that said: "Wipe Your Feet Before You Come In." This was in addition to the usual signs throughout the building about turning off the lights and putting towels in the wastebasket and: "Women's Rest

Room, 3rd Door on the Left," and signs over the sinks that read "Grace Is Free but Running Water Costs Money." There were also signs like: "Items Left in the Church More than 30 Days Will Be Disposed Of" and "Do Not Tamper with the Thermostats." Of course there were always signs in the rest rooms, which varied depending on the current condition of the plumbing. The signs would say things like "Hold the Handle Down Until the Flushing is Complete," or "Do Not Hold the Handle Down," or "Jiggle the Handle," or "Don't Jiggle the Handle." There was even a sign in the hallway, "Slower Traffic Keep Right."

When Hester Holloway put up a sign in the kitchen saying, "Feel Free to Take the Leftover Food" a sign appeared beside it the next week that read, "Do Not Leave Food on the Counter. There are Mice in Here." Hester posted another sign the week following, "Food Is Life and We Share Our Abundance." The next week by that sign there was a dead mouse with a sign saying "Overindulged on Abundance."

Signs in the church are not a good thing, especially with a rambunctious youth group. The signs got moved around. "Women's Rest Room, 3rd Door on the Left" for a while led to the pastor's study. "Items Left in the Church More than 30 Days Will Be Disposed Of" was posted on the pastor's chair behind the pulpit.

Otis insisted he was only trying to be helpful, but Otis, to put it bluntly, was a bachelor. He had no one to help him with—well, propriety. Soon after he became head trustee, back in the 1940s, Otis heard that the women's group was wanting to buy new dishes. Otis found a bargain on Esselburg Glass Company dishes and bought seventy-five sets, enough for the whole church. No one with a wife would have done that. The women themselves had spent four meetings debating on the style of the dishes they wanted and what matched the kitchen curtains. Under those circumstances, even the Queen's china, if not selected by the women themselves, would not have been acceptable for church dishes.

There was another time—I think this was in the 1950s—when Otis bought the church a ten-year supply of toilet paper. It seems that one year before Christmas someone in the Superior Paper Company over in Harrisville had a creative idea for a new product: toilet paper in colors of red and green with holly leaves and berries. The new product line was never marketed, for reasons Otis never investigated, and the company had a corner of their warehouse filled with cartons of Christmas toilet paper they were willing to move—cheap. Otis took advantage of that. The ten-year supply lasted one week. It seems the dyes in the paper were defective and when the product was used the colors ran. People in Hackleburg were certain the bubonic plague had struck when they discovered various parts of their bodies were streaked with red and green.

The year after the Christmas toilet paper Otis invested in casters. A semitruck full of industrial casters overturned on the other side of Pikeville, and Otis for the good of the kingdom negotiated another bargain. Casters from the Ace Ball Bearing Company in Chicago—cheap. Otis was tired of moving tables and pianos and pulpits around and casters seemed to offer a solution.

The next Sunday when Helen Bevins launched into an exuberant rendition of "I'll Fly Away" on the piano during opening exercises in Sunday school, the congregation was treated, if not to a flying piano, at least a sliding one. As the congregation sang, "When I die, Hallelujah by and by, I'll Fly Away," the piano, the piano bench and Helen herself were headed toward the side exit. Later in the service, when Pastor Bill Henry was preaching on the things of God that are immovable, he and his pulpit starting gliding toward the same exit, followed by the Communion table and the pulpit chair. A great deal of the furniture of the church, it seemed, started sliding one way or another. The church discovered which of their floors were not level. The youth group invited the Baptists over and they had a soap box derby with church tables down Evan's Hill over on Oak Street.

There was more. In the fall of 1956—it was the year Eisenhower was running for president—the We Care Sunday school class, in a burst of exuberance, purchased for the church a Manger Scene from the Real-Life Molding Company over in Harrisville. This company specialized in statues, monuments and figures made of plaster of Paris or cement for various customers: cigar stores, cemeteries, veterans' groups who wanted Union Army soldiers on Court House lawns, figures for carousels and monsters for haunted houses. Their outdoor Christmas sets never sold too well so one year they ran a special: three life-sized wisemen, four shepherds, two angels, a donkey, a camel, an innkeeper and wife, five sheep, Joseph, Mary, Baby Jesus and a manger, all for one low price of $599.

People had a few questions when the set arrived. One wise man looked suspiciously like a Cigar Store Indian, and a shepherd like a Union soldier, though he was holding a staff and not a gun. The innkeeper reminded them of Genghis Khan and the donkey like a carousel horse. They put up the whole set in the park pavilion, which doubled as a stable, got a lot of straw and even got some real live sheep to put in with the fake ones. They strung lights and played music. People came from all around to stand and sigh and talk about how wonderful it was.

But it was a lot of work, more than the We Care class had bargained for. The first year the figures were stored in the barn by January 2. The next year was a successful year—not so many people but still a good year. The figures got stored in the barn by January 25. There were fewer crowds the third year, and the figures did not make it into the barn until February 21. The fourth year things didn't go well at all. The spotlights kept blowing circuits. The real live sheep kept running away. The shepherds kept blowing over and Otis, park maintenance man as well as head trustee, had a lot of extra work. One night the Cigar Store Indian wise man and the Union Soldier shepherd were all that were attending Jesus in the manger, which was itself being drifted over with snow. People weren't saying, "How nice," but rather, "How weird." That year the set got put away by March 10.

The fifth year the excitement level was running low, except for the town dogs who showed up nightly to bark at the camel, the donkey and the sheep. The lights didn't work. There was no straw. By April when the grass began to get green people went by and saw sheep and the donkey and the camel out by the pavilion and believed the Hackleburg Park had become a pasture.

People still aren't sure whether it was Otis or the youth group, but at the Easter sunrise service that year the worshipers who came at dawn to celebrate the empty tomb realized some Bible characters had arrived before them. Mary sat on the front pew. The Genghis Khan innkeeper stood behind the pulpit, and the Cigar Store wise man stood where the ushers usually did with bulletins in his hand. In the choir loft were the innkeeper's wife, the rest of the shepherds and wise men and one camel. The other sheep and the donkey that resembled a carousel horse were in the Jesus' Little Sunbeams' class room to the grand delight of all of the sunbeams.

Soon after that, in biblical language, the people began to "murmur." Hadn't Otis been a trustee for a long time? Wasn't there something in the Methodist rules about a term of office? Otis didn't help matters when he found another good bargain, this time on purple and pink paint. One

Sunday people showed up for Sunday school and every-thing was purple and pink. After that, sometime in 1973, people began using a word that was rather rare around Hackleburg, the word "change." Time for a change. No-body wanted to tell Otis, so the new pastor, Pastor John Barryhill, was approached with a "preacher responsibil-ity." Preachers at Hackleburg come and go so they get asked to do things other people won't handle. Pastor Barryhill's task was to tell Otis it was time for someone else to be head trustee.

Pastor Barryhill used all his seminary training and his experience when he ran a plumbing business before he en-tered the ministry to approach Otis about how the church had a new challenge for him. They wanted him to be head of the Missions Committee. Of course the Missions Com-mittee had not functioned for ten years, a point Otis made to the pastor. But Pastor Barryhill had an answer for that: "All the more reason for you, Otis. We need someone cre-ative to get something going." Then Pastor Barryhill pulled out his ace in the hole (a figure of speech normally not used at Hackleburg church): Helen Dorris was asking the church to send a missions team to Bolivia. Helen was a missionary, the head of a children's hospital there. She had grown up in the Hackleburg church and had always en-couraged the church to get more involved in missions. If Otis would go visit the hospital in Bolivia, the church would pay his way.

Otis had never been out of the country and in fact had hardly ever been farther away than Harrisville, had never flown in an airplane and was really not interested in going to some place where he might be attacked by poisonous snakes. What would he do there? Furthermore, Otis was not easily fooled: this was a plot to get him out of his trustee's job, which for most of his life had kept him connected to the church and was basically his calling.

Otis went into a two-day depression. On the third day he received a letter from Helen in Bolivia:

Otis, they told me you might come to be with me at the hospital. I am so thrilled, not just for the sake of the hospital, but for the chance to see you again. We need you. I need you. There is so much you could do here. I have been praying about this and I am convinced this is God's will opening up in ways I could not have imagined.

Otis had never gotten very many letters in his life, especially letters from women, especially from a woman like Helen. It stirred in him a feeling he had never wanted to admit to anyone, including himself. He always liked Helen. They grew up together. She was one person he felt comfortable talking to. He had been at church camp with Helen— years ago—the night she felt called to the mission field. Otis had shook his head with a kind of personal disappointment—a tremendous girl like Helen throwing her life away to go to some far-off country instead of staying home and getting married. Now this same woman fifty years later wanted him to come visit her.

So Otis went to Bolivia, to the hospital for children that Helen ran. That was April of last year. Otis found a lot of things to do. The children needed a playground. Otis put up a big slide and called it Mount Sinai. He fashioned a merry-go-round and called it Elijah's Chariot. He painted rooms purple and pink and fixed a sandbox. He put casters on things. People loved the casters. He wrote signs in Spanish to put in the restrooms and on hospital walls. He fixed plumbing and did electrical wiring. The people loved it. Helen loved it. Otis became a hero.

More importantly Otis met a lot of new people with names like José and Marietta. He saw children get well in the hospital. He learned some Spanish words and tried to speak them, and everyone laughed. He saw people clap their hands when they worshiped. Otis began to wonder why the Hackleburg church had not shown more interest in Helen and this hospital.

He spent a lot of time with Helen. They would talk about Hackleburg, about Lush Larkin, Susanna the Methodist dog and church camp. They talked about the hospital and how the people of the hospital didn't want Helen to leave though she was old enough to retire. They talked about Jesus, which was sort of a new thing for Otis, even though he had been in the church for sixty-five years. They talked about the will of God. Helen shared her dream of a new wing for the hospital and new equipment, but she supposed she would never see it. It would cost $250,000 and $250,000 might as well have been ten million dollars.

Otis developed a burden, a good old-fashioned evangelical burden. During all of his years in the church he had never had a burden, a hurting for people to know God. He began to talk in ways that he had never done before. He talked about the will of God. He admitted he was disappointed the church no longer wanted him to be a trustee but maybe it was God's will. Maybe it was best they didn't want him as trustee any more, because if they hadn't wanted a different trustee he never would have come to Bolivia, and he never would have visited the hospital and Helen. Otis began praying about these things, which was something new because for all his church involvement Otis hadn't done much praying.

One night when Otis was praying about the will of God, Otis had a dream. In his dream he saw what appeared to be a redheaded angel driving an old car, no, not an old car, but a new old car. It was a Duesenberg, and the car was flying toward a hospital, and he was in the back seat and Helen was with him.

Well in September Otis got back to Hackleburg. He had stayed five months in Bolivia instead of two. People actually got a little worried about him. Otis called up Pastor Barryhill and asked if he could meet with him and maybe some of the church leaders on Tuesday evening. On Monday and on Tuesday before the meeting Otis was seen taking things out of the barn. Old tires, papers, broken-down lawn mowers. A green car had pulled up in the afternoon with Pikeville license plates, but no one thought too much about it.

Tuesday he went to the meeting. Pastor Barryhill was there, as was Hester Holloway who ran the kitchen, Connie Ashton of the Women's Group, Roy Hintley, the Sunday school superintendent, Aunt Minnie Rittenhouse who did children's work and Arthur Vanderweiss who handled finances and looked after the choir. They all wondered what the meeting was about.

Folks in Hackleburg are not easily shocked. For one thing, things are so predictable in Hackleburg that shocking things simply don't occur. It is hard to get shocked when you know exactly what people are going to say and do before they say and do it. But that night, at that meeting with Otis, the leaders of the Hackleburg church were shocked speechless. They were even dumbfounded.

Otis was a man of few words, and he got right to the point. He gave the pastor a letter of resignation as the head trustee. He had already begun to clean out the barn. He would not, however, be head of the Missions Committee.

Connie Ashton's eyes widened, "Why, Otis?"

"Well, because I don't figure to be around Hackleburg."

Minnie Rittenhouse pondered. This was not like Otis. She could not imagine Otis functioning in any other place except Hackleburg.

"What will you do, Otis?" Minnie asked.

Otis said, "Well, I am going to get married."

Arthur Vanderweiss, wise and caring older man, got alarmed. As far as he knew, and he knew a lot of things, there weren't any marriage prospects who would be interested in Otis. In the fifty years that he had known Otis, Otis had never expressed an interest in marriage or in women of any kind. Who would have him? Otis was having illusions.

"Well," said Arthur carefully, "this is something. Who to, Otis?"

"Well," Otis said, "to Helen, who did you think? You see, I've been called to be a missionary to Bolivia, to the hospital there. God called me. They have great needs there. They need a new wing and new equipment."

Now it was Pastor Barryhill's turn to be alarmed. He had had training about dysfunctional people who appear to be normal one day and then snap. Otis was his first case. Pastor Barryhill also knew about mission boards. As a very practical matter, no mission board would ever take a sixty-five-year old man who had no training and few social skills to be a missionary.

"Otis," said Pastor Barryhill, "it is a marvelous thing to be called, but how will you be supported? Who will send you?"

"The Holy Spirit will take care of it," said Otis. "I don't need a mission board. I'll just go."

The thought passed through several minds that in five months Otis had become a religious fanatic and had lost all sense of reality.

"Of course," Otis said, "I'll need your help and your permission. I figure I'll need $250,000."

They were now beside themselves. This was a downhill slide into chaos. Otis had never asked for help and for sure he had never asked anyone for permission. And $250,000 was like asking for ten million dollars. They could hardly even conceive of such an amount.

"In what way do you want our help, Otis?"

"I want the barn for missions."

"The barn?" Several persons replied in unison.

"Things like the Duesenburg and the stuff from the Variety Store."

A light bulb lit up in Arthur Vanderweiss' mind. Either Otis was completely deranged, or God was about to do a great thing. Arthur, a wise man of faith, from somewhere in the back of his mind remembered that Lush Larkin had once said he was going to buy a Duesenburg. If that Duesenburg were still around . . .

Arthur spoke first: "Show us, Otis."

Otis figured it would come to this, and he was ready. Otis led the little procession out of the church across the edge of the park and past some of the old tires and papers that had been removed from inside the barn. He opened the door and turned on the lights, and there in the corner was the Duesenburg, a 1932 Sports Coupe, gleaming in the light.

They believed. In a moment the skeptics believed. Aunt Minnie Rittenhouse whispered, "Mercy." Roy Hintley said, "Well, I'll be . . ." Pastor Barryhill said, "Praise the Lord."

Connie Ashton asked, "How much is it worth, Otis?"

"I don't know," said Otis, "but let me show you some more. Remember Johnson's Variety Store that used to be on Main Street next to Lush's Café during the Depression? Lush owned that building and when they went bankrupt Lush got all the merchandise as a result of the settlement."

Behind the Duesenburg in the old horse stalls were boxes stacked to the ceiling. There were knives and dolls in boxes and crates of patent medicines and forty-year old new appliances.

The green sedan that had been parked by the barn that day belonged to Glen Stover of the Stover Auctioneering Company out of Pikeville. Glen had not been too excited about handling an auction of a barn filled with junk and was ready to turn the auction down when Otis first called him. Until, that is, Otis mentioned a Duesenburg. Glen decided to take the auction. He told Otis they could probably have an auction some Saturday in November before it got too cold. They would put an ad in the Pikeville paper and might get a pretty good crowd, especially if they had an old car.

Then Glen came over. A Saturday auction in November with an ad in the Pikeville paper suddenly became a two-day auction in March with an ad in the Pikeville and Harrisville papers. That was before Glen saw the boxes in the horse stalls. Then it became a three-day auction in July with a full page ad in the *Antique News*, not just in the regional section but in the national section.

Every small town needs something every so often to come along and kind of perk it up and give the people something to talk about. What they discovered in that barn was good for six months of conversation. There was no wanting for volunteers to help clean the barn and sort the junk, only it wasn't junk now, it was antiques.

The Duesenburg had a total of fifty-six miles on the odometer, the exact distance from Harrisville to Hackleburg by way of Pikeville. In the glove compartment were some twenty-dollar gold pieces that Lush had evidently accidently left in there. There were seventy-five sets of dishes from the Esselburg Glass Company. There was an old Victrola with a record of "When They Ring Them Golden Bells." There was an old Civil War Springfield musket rifle. Someone had found it at the bottom of Henderson's Pond and had traded it to Lush for drinks, and Lush had had it restored.

The biggest job was going through all the papers. They put together sets of the *Harrisville Times* through World War II. They found old magazines: *Auto Mechanics, Look* magazines, *Life* magazines, *Woman's Home Companion, Coon Hunters' Digest*. They found comic books: Every Captain Marvel, Mickey Mouse and Lone Ranger comic book back in the 1930s.

The auction was held July 15, 16 and 17. There were more people in Hackleburg than Hackleburg had ever seen, with license plates from New York and California and Pennsylvania. Otis was everywhere for all three days of the auction. He greeted people, answered questions and joked about how God changes junk to riches. He was so full of energy that several of the widow ladies lamented to themselves that they had so quickly passed over Otis as marriage material.

People bought all the dolls from the variety store and watches and pocket knives and toy cars in boxes and patent medicine and brand new forty-five-year-old lunch boxes and the magazines and the papers and the comic books. They bought a nearly new deluxe set of J. T. Newcomb World War II set of soldiers, complete with German and British and Japanese armies that once had been in Jesus' Little Sunbeams' sandbox. They bought the valuable depression glass sets of dishes from the Esselburg Glass Company. They bought the Happy Hills Farm Set of little animals that dated from Depression days. They bought the red and green toilet paper with the holly imprint. Two wax museums, a carnival and a Bibleland tourist park got into a bidding war for the Real-Life Molding Company Christmas set with the wiseman that looked like a Cigar Store Indian. Someone bought the casters. A number of people bid on the old church pews that had been stored away since 1911. They bought old Communion sets and Bibles.

They bought the furniture out of Otis' house, not that that brought too much. Finally they bought the barn itself. It was thought to date from the 1850s and had huge axe-hewn poplar beams and wooden pegs. Bill Beckley had bought the field beyond the park and was going to fix up the barn and use it for show horses.

Well, the auction netted $253,043.14. On the Sunday before Otis left for Bolivia he gave a personal witness in church, which is something the old Otis would never have done. He talked about a God of surprises, a God who calls people for great things and how sometimes we get stuck in ruts doing things. And if he and Helen ever got too old to work down there in Bolivia they would come back. Maybe the church would need some signs in the rest rooms.

CHAPTER ELEVEN

Why It Rained the Day of the Sunday School Picnic

September 10, 1950

It rained yesterday, which is good for the corn, although the farmers have been complaining about too much rain. It rained a lot, nearly an inch and a half by Lester Kingseed's rain gauge. It sort of spoiled the Hackleburg Rally Day and Sunday school picnic that was held over at the park. That's too bad because the annual Sunday school picnic is a big event at Hackleburg. The visiting and feasting and socializing bring people together. It was important enough that a number of people had made it a matter of prayer. They prayed for good weather and a successful picnic, and when it rained they complained: "We've had enough rain for the corn; you would think God would honor our requests for a nice day."

While the Heavenly Father doesn't feel a need to defend weather matters, or explain why prayers are or are

125

not answered, Freddy, the Reluctant Angel, does get defensive about such things. He doesn't know if it will make people any happier, but he tries to explain.

It seems there is a prayer machine up in heaven that analyzes and sorts out prayer requests according to James 5:16, King James Version (the English translation they use in heaven): "The effectual, fervent prayer of a righteous man availeth much."

Freddy says that a number of prayers came in. Pastor Harding's prayer, for example. Pastor Harding, a truly righteous man by the prayer-machine standards, made two audible requests for a "nice day" for the picnic, though, Freddy admits, the pastor's fervency level was about 17 percent. While Pastor Harding favors a successful picnic, he also remembers the pop fly that he misjudged that bounced off his head during the softball game at last year's picnic and the resulting snickers. That thought definitely effected his fervency level. His prayers—one at the men's prayer breakfast, where he felt sort of obligated, and one during his pastoral visit to Minnie Skivers, where he ran out of other things to pray for—were mostly in the line of professional duty.

Herbert Riggs, Sunday school superintendent, prayed several times, with a high fervency level of about 92 percent, but there was a question about how "effectual"—that is, toward the end of good effects—his prayers were. All of life is a game with Herbert, and it is well-known that he had wagered a banana split with Ed Holman, superintendent over at the Baptist church, as to which church would have the biggest crowd at their picnic. The Baptists, on Labor Day, had 128. Herbert's goal was 129.

Aunt Nellie Wilcox also prayed, every morning in fact, for "blue skies and bright sunshine." Freddy allows that while the prayer computer did not exactly discount Aunt Nellie's requests, it noted that Aunt Nellie, resident saint not withstanding, had prayed every single morning for the last twenty-five years "for blue skies and bright sunshine," and if all her prayers had been answered, it would not have rained for a quarter of a century and all of Hackleburg Township would be a desert.

Janie Teegarden, high school junior, had a number of secret wishes and several hidden desires for a "warm day" so the softball game could be played. Last year Janie was the very first person chosen for teams, and she got on base every time she came up for bat, even when she struck out and the catcher dropped the ball. Her blue halter top and short shorts were washed and laid out.

Fuzzie Foster, Nickie Slater, Emilio Gomez and Buster Halleshaven also managed to pray for the softball game, the weather and the picnic. Or at least they had been thinking about it for a number of months and the angels gave them credit for their thoughts as prayers and ran them through the prayer machine. Last year the boys remembered Janie Teegarden had worn her green halter top and short shorts for the softball game. Freddy pointed out that the boys' fervency level was not bad, but their standing as "righteous men" was in question.

There were other prayers. Mahilda Brew, whose favorite contribution to the Sunday school potluck, homemade bread, gets soggy in wet weather, prayed. As did Maryjo Andrews, for whom wet weather means frizzy hair. Joe Fields, Sunday school teacher over at the Baptist church, prayed for very hot weather and a big crowd for the Methodists. Joe runs the ice cream parlor from which the Methodists had ordered their ice cream. Even Gertrude, Pastor Harding's dog, in her own way, knowing that something big was coming up, wagged her tail a lot and the angels put that through the prayer machine, too. Last year when it was hot Gertrude licked up a lot of spilled ice cream.

Against this outpouring of prayer for dry weather there was only one dissenter. Eddie Jarrett, age six, had invited his friend, Billy McPherson, to the picnic. Billy, who had no Sunday school experience, said he might be able to attend; his parents had planned a trip to the lake that day except they wouldn't go if it rained. So Bobby prayed for rain and mentioned to the Heavenly Father that maybe if Billy came to the picnic he might become interested in Sunday school.

The day of the picnic brought pouring rain and temperatures in the low 60s. Only fifty-three people made it to the pavilion in the Lush Larkin Hackleburg Memorial Methodist Episcopal Glory to God Bible Wonderland Hollyhock Municipal Park. Mahilda Brew's bread was soggy and Maryjo Andrew's hair was wild. Ed Holman called Herbert Riggs about his banana split. Janie Teegarden wore baggy jeans and none of the high school boys showed up. Nobody played softball. Most of the ice cream was sent back to the ice cream parlor.

Those who came huddled around the fireplace in the pavilion and made cracks about why didn't the Lord send rain the day the Baptists had their picnic since Baptists like water so well. Then they laughed and told stories about Methodists and Baptists and Catholics and what it must be like in heaven. Little children couldn't play on the swings so they talked to grandmas and grandpas about pets and school and making their beds in the morning. Pastor Harding started some choruses and people sang a long time.

That night the weatherman on the radio explained that an unforeseen cold front had moved in bringing unexpected rain and even weathermen can't be right all the time. Billy McPherson told his mother about the Methodist picnic, about the fire in the fireplace, the soggy bread, how grandmas had talked to him and how they sang songs. Then he said he would like to learn about Jesus and asked if he could go to Sunday school with his friend Eddie Jarrett the next Sunday.

CHAPTER TWELVE

Billy McPherson

October 3, 1995

They held Roy Hintley's funeral over at the church last Wednesday. Roy was ninety-two years old. He spent a lot of those ninety-two years as Sunday school superintendent of the church. He inherited the job. His mother was a Littlejohn, you know.

Hackleburg has had several preachers in the past who had the idea of a two-year term, or a three-year rotation, for church officers. You don't see that in the Bible. You mix people up and put them in jobs God never intended for them to have and you have disaster on your hands. As far as the people of Hackleburg are concerned, Roy was ordained by God to be Sunday school superintendent. That was his calling in life. You don't mess around with that. Those preachers who talked about two-year terms found out about two-year terms all right—theirs. Preachers move on. People stay.

So Roy passed away. Roy was a grand old saint. Bull-headed at times. Opinionated, but covered by the blood of Jesus. If they have any Sunday schools to run up in heaven, Roy will do the job.

Dr. J. William McPherson came back for Roy's funeral. Dr. McPherson, or Billy, as he is known by everyone around Hackleburg, is a local boy. He made it big when he left Hackleburg, to everyone's surprise. He pastors the big church over in Harrisville. Some say he would make a good bishop. People knew they hadn't heard the last of Billy when he left town. It's just that they didn't expect him to be—well, re-spected. One day a few years back Edna Callaway was in a church meeting over at Harrisville and heard people talk about Dr. McPherson and what a great man of God he was, a community leader and things like that. Edna came back and told that all over town. People had a big laugh. Their Billy—a "respected community leader"? No one ever an-ticipated that.

Except for Roy Hintley. Roy always did believe in Billy. "God will use you some day, son." That's what Roy would say. People remember his saying that a number of times. So Billy was close to Roy, and that's why Billy came back for the funeral.

Billy got started in the Hackleburg Sunday school when he was just a little kid. No one knew exactly how or why except that he was a friend of Eddie Jarrett. People suspect Billy's mother sent him to get him out of the house. You could see why. Billy was always into things. Always active. Some say hyperactive. He was single-handedly responsible for causing Sunday school teacher burnout in four or five of Hackleburg's best.

He was also the kid who sent the sandbox into exile, at least one of the times it went into exile. A lot of people know that story about the sandbox and the toy soldiers and Jesus' Little Sunbeam's Sunday school class.

It all started shortly after World War II when the Alfred Buntley family bequeathed toy soldiers to the kindergarten class; actually, what happened was that Gertrude, Ralphy Buntley's mother, was tired of having those soldiers underfoot and loaded them up one day and took them down to the church. It was a deluxe set of J. T. Newcombe World War II toy soldiers, with Japanese, German, British and American battalions, generals, sergeants and privates, along with antiaircraft guns, bombers and tanks.

They were a great sensation in the Jesus' Little Sunbeams' class. They didn't necessarily enhance the Sermon on the Mount and the idea of turning the other cheek, but they kept a bunch of little boys coming to Sunday school, including Billy.

They also caused some problems for Aunt Minnie Rittenhouse, teacher of Jesus' Little Sunbeams, when she tried to read stories from her Big Blue Bible Story Book. With all those soldiers around, kids were always wanting to fight World War II all over again. So Aunt Minnie got the idea one day (I think she read it in some book from Nashville) that kids should act out Bible stories with creativity, using whatever is available in the classroom. In the case of Jesus' Little Sunbeams' class that was, of course, the toy soldiers, along with a set of Happy Hills Barnyard Animals that Dorothy Slusher's parents donated when Dorothy went off to college. They figured she wouldn't need the little barn and fences and pigs and cows in the Kappa Phi Kappa sorority, so the church got them. They don't buy toys at Hackleburg. They live off donations.

So the kids acted out stories with the sandbox and the toy soldiers and the barnyard animals. The American general would play the part of Jesus. The American soldiers the disciples. The German soldiers would be the scribes and the Pharisees. The Japanese soldiers would be the Amalekites or sometimes the Baptists.

So of course kids had their own versions of the stories, like the story of the Good Samaritan. What fascinated them was the part about the guy getting beat up and left for dead. In their version he got beat up a whole lot more than Aunt Minnie thought was necessary. He got shot down by the Japanese antiaircraft guns, bombed by German planes, and run over by British tanks. If there was ever a guy that needed a Samaritan it was he.

Billy saw more possibilities in those stories than some of the others. When Aunt Minnie got into the story of Moses and the plagues, Billy brought some extra props. He got into his mother's cupboard and brought red cake coloring for when the Nile turned to blood. He put that coloring into whatever water was available in the church, including the stools in the restrooms. It scared the adults to death; they thought the town water system had gone berserk. And he brought some frogs for the plague of frogs and lightning bugs for the gnats.

For the plague of the firstborn he brought out the British army. They wiped out not only the firstborn but practically the whole Egyptian nation. I mean the avenging angel got them with tanks and guns and the works, barnyard animals getting slaughtered right and left. The kids got so fired up that when Sunday school was out they went over and took care of the Baptists as well as they were getting out of church. Snowballed them. Otis Hankins and the trustees weren't too happy, let alone the rest of the church, plus the Baptists. Roy Hintley defended Jesus' Little Sunbeams. Creativity. Otis Hankins thought they could do with a little less creativity and a bit more discipline.

The Sunday that Aunt Minnie got stuck in the snow and didn't make it to Sunday school Jesus' Little Sunbeams decided to do a story on their own—Noah and the Ark, unsupervised. They got the barnyard animals into the barn, which was the ark. They had to take the sand out of the sandbox.

Not knowing where to put it they poured some of it in that big hole on top of the piano. Then they began carrying pans of water from the girls' rest room for the flood, so they could drown all the leftover barnyard animals and the soldiers, British, Germans and whoever else, the Amalekites and the Baptists. Well, the sandbox overflowed. A flood over all the earth is not going to be contained in a sandbox.

Finally, somebody came to check after water dripped through the floor down into the basement where the Come Join Us class was meeting. Carlisle Peterson was teaching on Elijah and how it rained from heaven. That was the exact moment when water from above started dripping on his bald head. So the sandbox went into exile. Not even Roy Hintley could save it that time. A whole generation of Hackleburg kids missed the sandbox. That was the early 1950s. They didn't get that sandbox out again until the early 1960s.

In the meantime Billy and his friends had graduated from Jesus' Little Sunbeams and were ready for a new challenge, which was the acolyte program. Rev. Hatfield was right out of seminary and he had this idea, which he must have learned in seminary, about having acolytes. Makes things more worshipful. Hackleburg folks thought it was about the dumbest idea they ever heard. They had never had candles in that church, never wanted to be Catholic, so why start now? But Roy Hintley saw some possibilities. The liturgical significance didn't impress him at all, but he thought it might keep those kids interested. If you could get Roy convinced, he could convince the rest of the church. That's how Hackleburg became liturgical.

It did make a difference in worship. You put Billy and a couple of his friends in those robes and set them loose with real live fire, there's not a lot of talking in the congregation before worship. You watch to see what would happen this week. Maybe someone would trip over a robe and go sprawling. Or knock a candle over. Once when Billy was mad at

Willie Harbaugh, he just konked him with the candle lighter on the way up the aisle. Once he caught the altar scarf on fire. People paid attention because they never knew when they might have to run for their lives. More prayers were being offered than ever before.

But it was good for Billy. It got him interested in pomp and circumstance and the Old Testament. He read about festivals and processions and Levites and circumcision. The circumcision part he explained in detail to Clarabell Ingram and the fourth grade Sunday school class, to her horror. Clarabell thought they ought to get away from circumcision and the Old Testament and into something more edifying, like the Good Samaritan.

So they moved from circumcision to whether animals go to heaven. Billy was convinced the answer was yes, but of course they all knew that to go to heaven you had to get saved, and the only way to get saved was to be in church. That's how Billy's dog, Pasquel, Donna Turkington's cat, Buppy, and Willie Harbaugh's hampster ended up in the side room off the sanctuary the Sunday that Mabel Hesterly sang "Whispering Hope" as a solo, except it wasn't a solo. It was a duet: Mabel and Pasquel, Billy's dog. "Whispering Hope" was neither whispering nor hopeful.

Some trustees wanted to have a church trial, right on the spot. They didn't know how long animals had been coming to church. But Roy Hintley intervened. "At least these kids got somebody here. How many of you have a burden for the unsaved? How many people have you brought to church?" Put them right in their place. Nothing like a little guilt trip to quiet down a board meeting.

After Billy had been an acolyte for several years they made him a team captain. He was always the most enthusiastic acolyte the church had, so they just put him in charge of the whole thing when he was a seventh grader. He recruited and trained all the little kids.

And he expanded the whole show. He visited some church where they carried a cross, so Hackleburg started carrying the cross. Then they added the Bible, then the American flag and the Christian flag, then the offering plates, then they carried in the flower vases. They had a whole regiment marching up there. And they marched. Acolyte cadence. Left face, hep, hep, hep, hep. He had the organist play, "Onward, Christian Soldiers." Roy's wife sewed little monk outfits for the whole crew. People called it "The march of the monks."

The preacher wasn't sure he ever learned about that in seminary. Some other folks said it seemed awfully Catholic to them, but Roy Hintley defended it. He threw II Chronicles 4 and 5 at them. Right in the board meeting. Asked them if they had read II Chronicles 4 and 5 recently. Joe Lembright allowed he hadn't read it for a week or two, so Roy gave them some exegesis about Solomon's procession in the temple with the Levitical priests and their sons and kinsmen in fine linen garments with harps and lyres and one hundred and twenty trumpeters, carrying snuffers, basins, fleshhooks, firepans and holy vessels. That seemed a lot better way to prepare for the presence of God than simply having the preacher walk in dressed in a blue blazer and white socks. That settled it. What can you say to that? I mean it is the Bible.

Some people thought that when Billy got older he would settle down and get more sense. They were wrong. It was when Billy was a junior, in the youth group, that they decided one Christmas to sell Uncle Henry's Original Down-Home Holiday Fruitcakes as a money-maker. Billy did the ordering. He figured they could sell about 400. Most families in Hackleburg would buy them for Christmas presents and would take three or four. But Hackleburg isn't much for store-bought fruitcakes, and they sold only thirty-three. They had 367 fruitcakes left over.

The church got the bill, and there wasn't any money to pay for them except in the trustee's maintenance fund, which didn't make Otis Hankins happy one bit. They had to put out an appeal: Anybody that had a freezer had to take ten fruitcakes home and store them.

The year after the fruit cakes the youth group volunteered to do the Christmas program. Clarabell Ingle usually did it, but she was tired and since no one else volunteered to head it up, the youth group took it on. Rather Billy McPherson took it on. It would be an original production.

Billy started by recruiting the high school pep band. Then he borrowed the pom-poms from the cheer block at school and scenery left over from the last high school play, which was Romeo and Juliet. He lined up the third and fourth graders to do a bunny hop for Jesus and the fifth and sixth graders to do a Herald Angels pom-pom routine. The seventh and eighth graders were to play "Silent Night" on Coke bottles. He had a big ball of tin foil for the star and borrowed a search light from the Pikeville airport to highlight it. He got two sheep for the manger scene and wood chips for bedding. He had Donna Turkington for Mary, Willie Harbaugh for Joseph and Donna's sister Heather, age eighteen months, for Jesus.

The night of the program the church was packed. People weren't going to miss this for anything. High school kids and even Baptists showed up. They weren't disappointed. Everything went wrong. When they hooked up the searchlight to shine on the star, it blew every fuse in the church. They had to do the rest of the program by candlelight.

The pep band was supposed to do a Christmas song for the wise men, but they couldn't read their music, so they played one of the few songs they knew from memory, which was "Stars and Stripes Forever." A candle had to serve as the star, and Billy stood on a table and held it up with one hand. It was in front of the American flag, and someone said he looked like the Statue of Liberty and they didn't know what holiday it was.

The other song the pep band knew from memory was the Hackleburg fight song, which they played when Mary was supposed to be delivering the baby. The sheep baa-ed and baby Jesus wanted her mommy, and the wood chips, which were wet, had fermented and smelled like silage— and so did the church for the next three months.

But nothing is ever a complete disaster at Hackleburg. It smelled like a stable. It was so dark the Romeo and Juliet scenery did look like Bethlehem. On that first Christmas Jesus probably did cry, and the sheep probably did "baa." At the end of the program the youth group said they were going to give everyone a present, and they did, a fourth of a fruit cake. Then everyone ran out of lines to speak so people sat there and thought about it all while the seventh and eighth graders played "Silent Night" on their Coke bottles. People were glad they came.

Well, folks remembered a lot of those things when Dr. J. William McPherson came back for Roy Hintley's funeral. Dr. McPherson was asked to say a "few words" at the funeral. Of course, Dr. McPherson is a preacher and preachers never just say "a few words." Dr. McPherson talked for a long time about growing up in the Hackleburg church, about how Roy Hintley became like a father to him since his own father hadn't done such a good job. He also talked about Aunt Minnie Rittenhouse and the sandbox and the acolyte program and the youth group and the fruit cakes. People laughed and laughed, and it didn't seem much like a funeral at all.

Then Dr. J. William McPherson said he never would have known Jesus if it had not been for Hackleburg and Roy Hintley and the sandbox. And for sure he never would have been a preacher. It was Roy who would tell him, "God will use you someday, son."

And that was good for the people of Hackleburg to hear. Like a lot of churches, they sometimes get down on themselves. They fuss and get their feelings hurt and wonder how God could ever work at a place like Hackleburg. But at Roy Hintley's funeral they were reminded that God did love them and sometimes the things they thought were problems were blessings in disguise.

They pondered these things and then thanked God for Roy, for Billy, for the sandbox, the acolyte robes and the fruitcakes and for "Silent Night" played on Coke bottles.

Acknowledgments

To the barn next to the church in Claypool, Indiana, which housed, unknown to almost everyone, in addition to other things, a 1939 Lincoln with 500 miles.

To Scully, a beloved community dog who, after she died in the 1890s, was stuffed and can be seen to this day in the Huntington, Indiana, city museum.

To Henrietta, Methodist dog.

To Bert Ritter, who lived next to the church in Hudson, Indiana, who while he was supposed to be dying, overheard members of his family dividing the inheritance. He got well, changed his will and gave his house and his properties to the church.

To Maria Woodworth, later Maria Woodworth-Etter, a well-known Pentecostal evangelist, who as a "trance" evangelist in 1884 held Union Meetings in Kokomo,

Indiana. After the meetings, 267 persons were baptized in the Kokomo Creek and a church, which later was known as St. Luke's United Methodist Church, was started. Maria Woodworth taught that believers should pray specifically for the desires of their hearts.

To Luther Lotz, who lived with two bachelor brothers, all known for their cursing and wayward ways, and who kept many pigs, plus a number of dogs, but who was converted and became a part of the Mt. Pleasant Church.

To the trustee at the Covenant Church in Illinois who put casters on things.

To the little short pew by the side door at Wesley Church, Union City.

To Pleasantdale United Methodist Church, Blackford County, Indiana, a legitimate thirteen-pie church.

To Margaret Turner, who ran the kitchen and organized the potlucks at Wesley Church, Union City, and her sister in spirit, Geneva Troxell, First Church, Greentown, Indiana.

To the hollyhocks around my grandfather's house and barn.

To a sandbox I faintly remember.

To some mission trips I have been on that changed lives.

To the real Michael Anderson, who was baptized.

To the youth group in LaGrange, Indiana, who after World War II, stored papers in a barn while waiting (unsuccessfully) for the price to go up.

To women's groups I have known.

To Sunday school picnics I have known.

To some choirs I have known and have even directed, being reduced to the ultimate indignity.

To the town park of Ashley, Indiana, and to Howie King who kept it.

To the slide that once existed in Lehman Park, Berne, Indiana, which seemed, at least to a kid, to be forty feet high.

To Zion United Methodist Church, Howard County, Indiana, which, over a number of past years, has raised over $375,000 for missions by selling junk.

To my son-in-law, Scott Whitaker, who is a coon hunter.

To the life-sized church manger scene belonging to Wesley Church, Union City, Indiana.

To the Variety Store in Union City, Indiana, that closed its doors during the Depression and opened them forty-five years later for a grand auction.

www.ingramcontent.com/pod-product-compliance
Lightning Source LLC
Chambersburg PA
CBHW072000170626
46813CB00005B/1940